#3

Danger Signals in Belize

Books by Maylan Schurch:

Justin Case Adventures:

JUSTIN CASE

#3

Danger Signals in Belize

MAYLAN SCHURCH

REVIEW AND HERALD® PUBLISHING ASSOCIATION
HAGERSTOWN, MD 21740

The author assumes full responsibility for the accuracy of all
facts and quotations as cited in this book.

This book was
Edited by Randy Fishell
Designed by Tina Ivany
Electronic makeup by Shirley M. Bolivar
Cover art by Thompson Bros., Inc.
Typeset: Cheltenham Book 11/16

PRINTED IN U.S.A.

06 05 04 03 02   5 4 3 2 1

R&H Cataloging Service
Schurch, Maylan Henry, 1950-
        Danger signals in Belize.

        I. Title.

                813.6

ISBN 0-8280-1613-5

Dedication

This book is dedicated to Onilee,

who played first base like she was born to it;

and to Penny and Chester,

who joined Onilee in playing baseball with me on our dry South Dakota farm creekbed, sometimes with a tightly rolled sock.

Acknowledgments

Thank you, *Guide* magazine editor, good friend, and perpetual idea fountain, Randy Fishell, for not only suggesting the basic plot kernel behind this story but shepherding me through to a publishable book.

Thank you, Ursula Towns, for all your helpful information about Belize. You're not responsible, of course, for the silly mistakes I might still be making about your mom's homeland.

And thanks to the Black Hills Health and Education Center in Hermosa, South Dakota, on whose cheerful August campus (in the cracks between five-mile walks, weight-room workouts, lectures, massages, contrast showers, the grim Russian steam cabinet, and lots of other body-toning activities) I wrote the first draft of this book.

Contents

CHAPTER 1

Screams at the Way Station

"We're landing, Justin," Rico Moreno said. "You can look now."

Thump. Squoook. Roaaarrrr. Rumble-rumble-rumble.

Justin Case, who hated flying, opened his eyes and cautiously stared past Rico out the jetliner's window at misty green trees whipping past them. "Awesome," he said.

"It's raining," Rico sighed.

"It's awesome—it's solid ground."

Rico snickered, then said, *"Bienvenidos a Belize."*

"What?"

"Sorry," Rico apologized. "Welcome to Belize. I was getting into my Spanish mode. Uncle Miguel's probably going to want to talk Spanish." He punched his friend on the knee. "Are you OK?"

"Ugh. Don't do that."

"Your face looks green."

"I'm OK," Justin insisted. "Just don't jiggle me."

"You've wadded your barf bag into a paper ball."

Justin grinned weakly. "Oh, yeah." He slipped the crumpled bag into the seat pocket in front of him. "Let's go." He got to his feet, wobbling a little, and grabbed his backpack.

Along with a lot of tourists, the two friends shuffled

their way down the plane's aisle. As they came through the gate into the noisy terminal, a short, stocky Hispanic man stared at them, then grinned and strode forward.

"Hola, Tio Miguel," Rico said politely, holding out his right hand. He nodded to his friend. *"Este es mi amigo Justin."*

"Rico, you rascal," the man said, "don't you know that Belize's official language is English?" He stepped back and squinted. "You *are* Rico, right?"

"Right," Rico replied with a smile.

Laughing with delight, the man lunged forward and gathered Rico into a huge hug. "Last time I saw you was in Mexico City, just before you and your sister and your mom headed for the States." He looked Rico up and down. "What are you now, 10?"

"Almost 13, same as Justin. This is Justin."

"Hi, guy." Rico's uncle grabbed Justin's hand in a healthy squeeze, then stared at Rico again. "Last time I saw you, you were a foot and a half long. And bawling like a baby."

"I *was* a baby, Tio Miguel."

"I guess you were, at that. Hey. Call me Uncle Mike. This is a veddy British countreh," he said in a fake English accent. "Believe it or not, my Spanish is getting rusty." Suddenly he glanced at his watch. "Whoa, the broadcast starts in a half hour."

"What broadcast?" Rico asked.

His uncle scanned the terminal with his eyes. "Didn't I tell you about that?"

"You told me you were going to teach me how to start a little radio station. I didn't know you were actually on the air."

"I'm supposed to be on the air in 30 minutes!" Suddenly Uncle Mike sighed. "I wonder if this was the best time to invite you down here. Things are getting a little bit weird. But hey, let's not talk about that. We've got to refuel. Ma'am?" he called to a woman who was strolling along with a metal box. "Over here, please. Three *panades.*" He gave her some money. "These are delicious," he said, handing two *panades* to the boys. "Refried beans inside a tasty bread wrapping. They're even better with Marie Sharp's hot sauce on them."

Uncle Mike gave a quick glance at Justin. "You OK with the *panade?* You're looking a little pale."

"Justin hates flying," Rico explained.

"I'm OK," Justin insisted.

"By the way, don't drink the tap water," Uncle Mike said. "I've gotten used to it after a couple of years, but was I sick at first! I've got cases of bottled water for you back at the Way Station."

He hurried them past several other people carrying baskets or boxes trying to sell things to arriving and departing tourists—stuffed animal jaguars, wood-carved tapirs, colorful wood back scratchers with "A present from Belize" printed on them, even some powerful Wrist Rocket slingshots.

"Wow," Rico said as they reached the terminal door. "It's really raining out there."

His uncle grinned. "Don't like the weather? Wait 15 minutes." He pushed open the glass door and took a deep breath. "Run!"

The three of them scampered across the parking lot, dodging puddles. Justin held his *panade* close to his body

as warm raindrops pelted against his face and hair. The car wasn't locked, so they heaved their suitcases inside and dove in after them, slamming the doors. The rain drummed steadily on the roof.

"This rain's a pain," gasped Uncle Mike, "but think of all the water barrels that are filling up. Every house has a water barrel in its backyard." He started the engine. "Sorry your sister couldn't make it, Rico."

"Tessa's sorry too," Rico responded. "But she just got a summer job."

"Thank you for letting me use her ticket, Mr. Moreno," Justin said from the back seat.

"Call me Uncle Mike," the man said, tossing a grin over his shoulder. "You're my official nephew while you're here. Got that?"

"Thanks, Uncle Mike."

"You're welcome. Glad you could come." Uncle Mike guided the car out of the parking lot, the windshield wipers whipping madly back and forth. "I've worked my schedule so that I can be around to take you places. We'll give you an interesting time."

And on certain frightening days that lay ahead, Justin would think of that statement over and over again.

*   *   *

The trip into Belize City was several miles, but it went incredibly fast because of Uncle Mike's stories and the beautiful green trees and colorful houses. Belize was tropical and glorious even in a rainstorm. A bus with the words *"Novelos"* and *"Benque"* on it passed them, filled with people.

But by the time they'd reached Belize City they'd driven out from under the weather. Nosing the car through a network of streets, Uncle Mike soon pulled up beside a magnificent old two-story building that looked part-mansion and part-hotel.

"This," he said proudly, "is the Way Station. Come on. Let's get your gear unloaded."

Justin and Rico grabbed their suitcases and backpacks. As they hurried up the walk, their attention was distracted by a large group of kids playing in the large vacant lot next to the building. Several adults were sitting in some bleachers watching them.

"Uncle Mike," Rico said, "that looks like a baseball game."

"It is. You sound surprised."

"I thought everybody down here played soccer."

"They do—they call it 'football.'" His uncle opened one of the Way Station's giant double doors and ushered them into a large lobby with several comfortable sofas in it. "Cricket, too, once in a while. But there's a lot of interest in baseball down here, since quite a few Central and South American guys are major-leaguers making big bucks in the U.S." Uncle Mike laughed suddenly. "Those kids out there are diehards. They play baseball Mondays, Wednesdays, and Thursdays—rain or shine. OK, let's head upstairs," he said urgently. "Two minutes to air time."

"Two minutes?" Justin stared. "The studio is here?"

"Yep, follow me."

Uncle Mike took the stairs two at a time, and the boys scampered after him. He fumbled with a ring of keys and inserted one into the large deadbolt lock of the second door on the left. He glanced back over his shoulder at an open door across the hall. "Hi, Isaac," he said to a tanned, gray-haired man who sat in the room reading a newspaper. "My two nephews."

The man smiled. "Hello," he said. "Welcome to Belize."

Uncle Mike led them inside and closed the door. "I keep this locked when I'm out," he muttered. "Because like I say, things are getting weird around here. I'm going to give each of you a key, and I want you to make sure you lock the door each time you leave. This room is also going to be your bedroom."

"This is great!" Justin said. "Bunk beds!"

"I get the top one," Rico said quickly. "You're scared of heights, remember?"

Justin groaned, then glanced around the room. "Where's the studio?" he asked.

"Right here," said Uncle Mike, pointing. "It's a low-power FM station. It reaches out only a couple of miles, but it covers a good chunk of Belize City. Lots of people listen every night for the two hours I'm on."

Against a wall, beside a window, stood a long wooden table with a chair facing it. At the right end of the table was a computer and printer. At the left end, closest to the window, sat two dark-green boxes with their lids off.

"FM broadcasting unit. Tape player," Uncle Mike said, pointing to them one by one. "And this big old silver radio is a multiband unit. Gets everything from AM and FM to short wave. I listen to myself on its earphones to see if I'm really broadcasting."

On the wall was a large brown bulletin board covered with papers and newspaper clippings, and higher yet hung a large electric clock. A large metal trash can with handles on the side stood beside the table. Taped to its side was a piece of white paper with red lettering: "HATE MAIL."

"You get hate mail?" Rico asked in a worried voice.

Uncle Mike chuckled. "Sometimes. That sign is half-joke, half-real. Most of what's in there is just junk mail I get. But a few people really don't like my little broadcast." His hands hovered expertly above the two electronic units and the old silver radio, flicking switches and turning dials. Needles jumped. Little red lights glowed.

He put on the earphones, sat down in the chair, and punched what looked like a PLAY button on one of the machines. He listened for a moment, then smiled. "My theme song," he chuckled. "'The Sound of Silence.' That's what some of my listeners wish I broadcasted—silence."

"Are you on the air now?" Justin whispered.

"I will be when I do this," Uncle Mike said, and he pushed a square black button. "Good evening, ladies and gentlemen," he said in a smooth announcer's voice into the microphone. His other hand turned a dial to the left, fading out the theme song. "Welcome to the most interesting two hours of radio in all of Belize. I'm happy to have with me in our studio my nephew Rico Moreno and his friend Justin, who have just arrived from the United States. We'll hear from them just a little later in the program."

The boys backed away in terror, shaking their heads. Uncle Mike just grinned. "I hope," he said into the mike, "that everybody enjoyed our rainstorms this afternoon. The weather forecaster says—"

Suddenly, from somewhere on the first floor came a loud, mournful wailing. Uncle Mike's eyes widened. He stabbed the square mike button to OFF. "What was that?" he asked sharply.

"A woman's voice," Rico said.

The distant wailing changed to screams.
"Mr. Moreno! Help!"

"It's Mary," Uncle Mike said. "What is going on?" He glanced rapidly around the room, then out the window to where the baseball game had just begun. Suddenly his eyes shone with delight. His finger hovered over the mike button again, and he stood up.

"Get over here, guys," he said. His finger landed on the button. "Ladies and gentlemen, you're in for an extra-special treat this evening. Outside my studio window here the Mayans and the Jaguars are just beginning what promises to be a great baseball game. And here for the play-by-play are Justin and Rico."

He thrust the microphone into Justin's hand, then ran for the door and disappeared as another scream echoed up from below.

CHAPTER 2

On the Air With Justin and Rico

Justin and Rico stared at each other open-mouthed.

"Uhhhhh . . ." Justin said into the mike, and to his horror one of the needles jiggled. He looked around in terror, then quickly stuck the mike under his left armpit.

"Yuck!" Rico gasped. "That's *your* mike from now on," he whispered. "I'm never going to use it. I hope you put on deodorant."

In panic, Justin scanned the buttons and lights. "Which one of these is the OFF button?" he asked.

"No!" yelped Rico, throwing his body over the controls. "Don't turn it off!"

"But I don't know what to say!"

"Do the game!"

Another scream from below, louder this time.

Forgetting that the mike was under his arm, Justin grabbed Rico with both hands and tried to pull him away from the controls. "How can I do the game? I don't know any of the—"

The mike, released from his armpit, began to fall. Justin reached down, caught it just in time, and clapped it under his armpit again. "I don't know any of the players!" he hissed. He tried to push Rico away from the controls.

"Justin, we've gotta do this."

"Why?"

"Think of all those people listening to the station."

"I don't care."

Another scream, followed by Uncle Mike's voice saying, "Watch out. Watch out!"

"What," Justin asked, "is going on down there?"

"That's not our problem," Rico said tensely. "Our problem is that Uncle Mike will get even more hate mail if his station doesn't make any sounds. And listening to your armpit," Rico continued, "is not very exciting."

Justin glared at him. "You do the game then."

"I'm not doing it."

Justin's eye fell on the huge clock. The second hand was turning. He took the mike from under his arm.

"Uh, good evening, ladies and gentlemen." He cleared his throat a couple of times. "I am sorry, but we've just been having some—" He stuffed the mike under his armpit again. "What, Rico? What are we having?"

"Panades?"

"No! What do stations have when they go off the air for a minute?"

"Oh. 'Technical difficulties.'"

Up went the mike. "We've been having technical, uh, dillicuffies," Justin said.

"Difficulties!" Rico corrected.

"Dilli-diffl—problems," Justin compromised cautiously. "Anyway, about the game. Mr. Moreno was called away suddenly and he didn't have time to tell us who the players were. But we'll do the best we can." Suddenly Justin had an idea. "Uh, I know some pretty good jokes. Here's one: A really greasy-haired guy came into the barbershop one day. The barber asked him, 'Do you want a haircut or just an oil change?'"

Rico looked over at Justin in horror.

"I know another one," Justin continued. "Did you hear about the kid who spilled root beer on the stove? Now he has foam on the range!"

Suddenly Rico whispered into Justin's ear, "Do the game, the game!"

Justin sighed, then stood up and peered out the window. "But now," he said into the mike, "let's check into the action on the field. Rico, it looks like a police officer is the umpire. And there's this tall guy up to bat now. Here's the pitch."

"Wow, look at that!" Rico said.

"It's a high fly ball, way out over the street!" Justin cried. "Look, Rico, it almost hit that car. The centerfielder is chasing it. Hey, she's a girl! I mean, well, you know . . . How can she run in that long dress? The batter is rounding second, on his way to third."

"He'll make it, easy," Rico chimed in.

"Home run!" Justin shouted. "I just wish we knew who he was, because it was a good home run. OK, the next batter comes up to the plate. Here's the pitch."

Justin heard the door open, and turned. A tiny elderly woman hobbled into the room, followed by Uncle Mike, who had a thoughtful look on his face. He ushered the woman over to the bunk beds and she sat on the lower bunk. Then he glanced at Justin, grinned, and gave a thumbs-up. Justin silently offered him the microphone, and he took it.

"Well, neighbors," Uncle Mike chuckled. "What do you think of our new play-by-play team? If you want this dynamic duo to continue as your broadcast team, just call the Way Station and leave a message on my machine."

One more time Justin and Rico stared at each other open-mouthed. Through the open door they could hear the telephone start to ring.

Uncle Mike glanced up at the big clock. "We'll be back to the game in a little bit," he said into the mike, "but I know you folks have been waiting for the BBC headlines. And meanwhile I'll be coaching the boys on who's who with the teams." He reached over to the giant radio and tuned it to another frequency. As it hissed and crackled, he rotated the dial and finally got a clear British voice. He adjusted the boom mike close to the speaker and then beckoned to the boys to follow him over toward the elderly woman seated in the room.

"I've got the biggest short-wave antenna in this part of town," he whispered to them as they crossed the room. "I can pick up the BBC better than anybody else in this area. Now, boys, this is Mary," he said. "Mary's been our guest for a month now. She's just had quite a shock."

Mary quivered all over. "It was just terrible," she said. "Horrible."

"But we got him," Uncle Mike reassured her. "Isaac is checking your room for holes, and if he finds any he'll plug them up. Mary found a rat in her room," he said to the boys. "A big brown hairy one. Wait a minute, Mary. I thought you grew up on a farm. You've seen rats before, haven't you?"

She nodded. "It's the rabies I'm afraid of. Some of them have rabies."

Uncle Mike shrugged. "Good point. Well, Isaac's going to make sure it doesn't happen again. Now," he said, shooing the boys over to the window. "We've got about six minutes left of BBC headlines. Get a piece of paper and take down the team lineups. I'll coach you if you forget names."

"Uncle Mike," Rico said respectfully but firmly, "I think you'd better find someone else to do the games. We've never done play-by-play before."

"Hey, all you need is a bit of information. Give it a try, just for today. OK, got that pencil ready? I know most of the kids. And I know the umpire, too."

"He looks like a police officer," Justin said. "Do police officers always umpire baseball games in Belize?"

Uncle Mike chuckled. "No, that's Trent Morgan. He's Calvin's father. Calvin's that tall kid. Hits a lot of home runs."

Once the BBC broadcast was over, Uncle Mike introduced the boys again. "I know," he said into the microphone, "that several of you have brought radio sets to the game to pick up my program as you watch. Is anybody listening out there in the bleachers? Raise your hand."

Five or six people glanced around at the window and waved.

"Thanks for listening. And now to start up the play-by-play again," said Uncle Mike, "here's Rico."

Rico shook his head. "Justin," he whispered.

"Rico. It's your turn."

"Calvin Morgan is at bat," Rico said with a sigh into the mike. "And now the pitch. Whoa! He squares to bunt . . . and pops it straight to the pitcher. Earlier in the game Calvin hit a long home run."

"He really had 'em surprised," Justin said, leaning toward the mike. "It looked like nobody expected Calvin to bunt. Even the infielders were 'way back. Too bad he couldn't lay it down. He would have made it to second."

*   *   *

"Well, what do you think, guys?" Uncle Mike asked as the game ended. Down on the field the players were giving each other high-fives. "Did you have fun? Just a little?"

Justin grinned and nodded.

Rico shrugged. "Yeah, I guess so. But it was like learning to swim by getting tossed into a lake."

"Whatever it takes," Uncle Mike chuckled. "Now, are you hungry?"

"Yeah!" said the boys together.

"Let's go downstairs. Mary, why don't you come eat with us?"

Mary's eyes widened in relief. "Oh, Mr. Moreno, that would be so kind."

"No trouble at all."

"I could fix you supper," the woman offered.

"No, no, Mary. Not necessary."

"Please," she insisted. "I cook for my grandchildren in the country. But here at the Way Station I have no one to cook for but myself. Please allow me."

After saying Hi to Isaac again, they descended the stairs. In the downstairs hall they saw three of the players heading toward the lobby door.

"Great game, guys," said Uncle Mike. "I let the players use the Way Station restrooms during the game," he told the boys.

Once in the cozy kitchen, Uncle Mike set the table while Rico and Justin helped Mary find a skillet.

"So you're here for a visit from the country?" Justin asked her.

"Not exactly," Mary said. "I have to go to the hospital every day."

"Mary's our guest while she's taking treatments," Uncle Mike said. He went to the refrigerator and took out a red bottle that looked like ketchup or hot sauce.

Mary nodded. "And I don't have to pay anything to stay here," she said, gratefully.

"A government grant pays for it," Uncle Mike said, setting the bottle on the table. "Mary's not exactly rich, and she doesn't have relatives here in Belize City. So if there were no Way Station, she'd have to rent a hotel room, which would be impossible. So she stays here. Rico, please fill four of those glasses with water."

"Sure."

"It's a beautiful old place," Mary said. "I've always loved it."

"Except for the rat," Uncle Mike reminded her.

She shuddered. "Yes. I hope Isaac finds the hole."

"That's funny." Uncle Mike clinked four forks down on the table and sat down in the chair closest to the window. "I was sure there weren't any holes in that room. This place is normally rat-free. But," and Justin could hear the seriousness in Uncle Mike's voice, "there are lots of other rats besides that one."

"Mr. Moreno!" Mary gasped.

"Human rats, I mean."

"Human rats?" Rico asked.

His uncle nodded. "They don't like the Way Station and what we're trying to do here."

"Who are they?" Justin asked.

"Drug dealers, mainly. Did you hear me do my war on drugs announcement up there? That's just the kind of thing the dealers don't like. They don't want people to think about the drug problem. And they don't want the average citizen to know that there's something he or she can do about it."

"Drugs are terrible," Mary said. A large supply of re-fried beans was sizzling in her skillet. "My grandson almost died from cocaine. I don't think he's using it anymore. But I am making sure."

Justin glanced at her, then at Rico. Rico was staring at her too.

"What's that, Mary?" Uncle Mike asked. "You're making sure?"

She nodded.

"How?"

She stirred the beans in silence.

"You don't want to talk about it?"

"You wouldn't understand, Mr. Moreno."

He straightened in his chair. "Not voodoo."

She didn't answer, but stirred harder.

"Mary, are you doing voodoo there in your room?"

Silence.

Uncle Mike got up from his chair and came over beside her. "Mary, you must not burn candles in your room. This place would be charcoal in 15 minutes if they started a fire. No candles, understand?"

"No candles," she promised. "But if I see more rats I will have to go back to the country."

"And skip your treatments?" he said. "You'd be worse off than you were before. Here, let me take over with the rice and beans. You've got to stay off your feet or you won't get better." Whoever deserved the credit, the rice and beans were superb. Justin had never really liked them, but tonight he ate three huge helpings.

"What's the name of this hot sauce?" he asked, reaching for the bottle and turning it to see the label.

"Marie Sharp's," Uncle Mike said. "It's made right here in Belize, and you can get it in other countries too. Pretty zingy, huh?"

Justin nodded. He was about to say something else when a buzzer sounded.

"Rico, someone's at the door," his uncle said. "Check it out, will you?"

Rico jogged out the doorway and down the hall. Justin heard a girl's voice. Then into the kitchen came the tall blond girl, named Hannah, followed by a very serious-looking Rico. Hannah smiled shyly at Justin, but as she turned to Uncle Mike her face went serious too.

"Mr. Moreno," she said. "Do you know about the window?"

He glanced up. "Window?"

She nodded. "When the game was done I went home to my aunt's house. But then I remembered I'd left the bag of groceries I'd picked up at the market before the game. I came back for it, and then I happened to look up at your window. You know, the one you do the broadcast from."

"What's wrong with the window?"

"It's smashed," she said.

CHAPTER 3

Home-Run Hannah

Uncle Mike pushed his chair back. "Smashed?" he asked.

"I didn't hear anything," Rico said.

"We probably wouldn't hear it," his uncle said. "The room is above us, but this is a thick old building."

"Maybe a bird hit it," Rico suggested.

Uncle Mike glanced at the ceiling. "That's probably what happened. He thought the reflection in the glass was a patch of clean sky, and *kabang!* Good thing you told us about it, Hannah. The guys and I will have to do a bit of cleanup before bedtime. Oh, let me introduce you to every-body."

As names were exchanged, Justin silently tried to guess Hannah's age. She seemed to be 13 or 14. The girl was tall and blond, and wore a long, light-blue dress, something like a prairie girl might have worn a century ago. The dress was a little smudged. Hannah's head was covered with a bonnet of the same color, tied under her chin. And her eyes were the same color as her dress.

"Justin Case?" she said with an unbelieving smile. "Is that your real name?"

"That's it," Rico spoke up. "He's lucky his parents didn't call him Book."

Justin waved a fist at his friend. "Don't pay any attention to Rico," he urged the girl. "He used to be in the circus."

She glanced at Rico with interest. "The circus?"

Justin nodded. "We used to come and visit him in his cage."

Hannah sputtered into laughter. "Well, I'd better be going."

"Stick around," Uncle Mike said. "Had supper yet?"

"Not yet, actually. But—"

Uncle Mike pointed to his chair. "I'm done. Sit down and I'll get you a new plate. Mary's rice and beans will fill you up, you hard-hitting centerfielder, you."

"I don't want to invite myself . . ."

"You didn't; I did. Just call your aunt and let her know where you are."

"Auntie's at a committee meeting at church," she said. "I shouldn't stay too long. But I was worried."

Uncle Mike began to dish up a new plate of rice and beans. "About what? Your batting average?"

"No, about your window."

"Why?"

"I mean," she said hesitantly, "you know how some people don't like your broadcast."

He plopped the plate in front of Hannah and nudged the Marie Sharp's hot sauce within reach. "Hey, stop worrying. While you're chowing down here getting acquainted with the boys, I'll run upstairs and check everything out. Mary, want me to walk you to your room?"

The little woman shook her head. "No thank you. I believe I'll go see what's on the telly in the lobby."

"Now just stop worrying, Mary. Understand?" She smiled doubtfully at him and hobbled through the doorway.

Hannah smiled too as she heard Uncle Mike bounding up the stairs. "I like your uncle," she told Rico. "How long has it been since you've seen him?"

"A long time ago. I was like 1½ years old."

"I hope he stays in Belize," she said. "We need him here."

Justin said, "Have you lived here all your life?"

Hannah nodded. "I was born on my father's farm out near Orange Walk."

"Rico's uncle said you were Mennonite."

She grinned and brushed at a dirt stain on her skirt. "That's right. You can always tell us by our long dresses."

"Why don't you wear jeans when you play ball?" Rico asked.

"Dad says it's not modest."

"How do you slide, then?"

Hannah giggled. "When I run, I lift up my skirt a little, to my knees. Same thing when I slide."

"But," Justin remarked, "you don't usually have to slide because you hit your home runs so far."

She blushed. "I get lucky once in a while." Then her face turned serious. "I'm really fortunate to be in town. Dad wishes I was back on the farm doing fieldwork, but Auntie wants me to help her here." She glanced at the ceiling. "I'm glad your uncle's radio station doesn't reach our farm."

"How come?" Justin wanted to know.

"Because if Dad heard all the things I was doing in the

game he'd drive right in and pick me up and take me away." She took a sip of water and stood up. "I'd better go. If Auntie gets home before I do, she'll worry."

After she'd gone, Rico said to his friend, "I'm going to check e-mail in Uncle Mike's bedroom. Come with me."

Justin shook his head. "I think I'll see what's on TV in the lobby."

As he wandered down the long hallway, he passed door after door. He could see cracks of light under most of them and occasionally hear a little radio music. Nobody seemed to have a TV of their own. He wondered who all the people were, and why they were staying at the Way Station, and why Uncle Mike loved being here so much.

And he wondered about the window.

Arriving in the lobby, he sat in a chair beside Mary. On the TV screen was an old-fashioned black-and-white pro- gram starring a man with dark hair and a deep voice.

"What program is this?" he asked.

"Perry Mason," she said. "A lot of our programs come from the U.S. This week the station is playing old Perry Mason reruns."

Justin settled down to watch.

An hour later, Rico stuck his head into the lobby. "Justin, I'm logging off in a minute. Last chance to check your e-mail."

"That's OK. I'll do it tomorrow."

"What's on?"

"Perry Mason," Justin said.

"Who's he?"

"I don't know."

"You must not be homesick," Rico said.

"Not yet. Are you?"

Rico shrugged and turned away.

It was late when Justin tiptoed into the darkened bed-and broadcast room.

"Justin?" Rico whispered.

"Yeah."

"Uncle Mike boarded the window up."

"What was it?"

"Not sure. A bird, he thinks. It made a big hole, but he didn't find anything in the room that could have come through from outside. We'll probably find a dead bird on the ground tomorrow."

"Great," Justin said sarcastically as he slipped between the bottom bunk sheets. "Just what I wanted to think about while I was going to sleep—dead birds. Thanks."

"You're welcome," Rico replied, shifting position. "As for me, I always pray that I'll have good dreams."

"I guess that's not a bad idea," Justin said. He made a mental note to try that kind of prayer. "Those boards on the window," he said suddenly. "Does that mean we won't have to call the game tomorrow?"

Rico yawned. "I guess we'll find out. You got some e-mail, by the way."

"Did you print it out?"

"Of course not; I wouldn't read your e-mail."

"Oh, OK."

"Good night," Rico said.

"Good night."

As he drifted off, Justin thought to himself, *Whoops. I forgot to pray. Dear Jesus* . . . And then he was asleep.

Justin dreamed that he was playing the bass drum in a marching band. He had not been able to find his band uniform so he had to stride down the street with nothing on but a pair of bright-red boxing trunks. Hannah was on the sidewalk watching him and screaming with laughter. *Bang . . . bang . . . bang . . .* He banged the drum louder and louder to try to distract her with music.

*   *   *

Bang! Bang! Bang! went the big bass drum.

"Guys! Wake up."

Justin rolled over and found that he wasn't playing a drum after all. Someone was knocking on the room's door.

"Rico, Justin. Get dressed. You've got company."

Rico tumbled off the top bunk and fumbled for his jeans. Justin, whose eyes were gradually opening, noticed bright daylight shining through the window boards.

"Come in," he called when he too was dressed.

The door opened, and in came Uncle Mike and a man they'd never seen before, broad-chested and red-faced and wearing farmer's overalls and a wide-brimmed hat.

"Aha," said the man with a wide smile and a German accent. "These boys need to come out on my farm. There we get up early."

"Good idea," agreed Uncle Mike with a chuckle. "Every

kid ought to have a summer's worth of farmwork under his belt. Seriously, guys, sorry to get you up. But this is Willy Straub, Hannah's father."

The boys blinked the sleep out of their eyes and said polite hellos.

"Yah," said Mr. Straub, walking over to the window and beginning to tug on the boards. "Hannah called on the telephone last night and said you had a window broke. I have just bought a lot of plexiglass, and I said, 'plexiglass is what that window needs.' That crazy bird. Why don't he think? No, he just go *zoop, zoop, zoop, whammo.*"

He yanked off two or three boards. "Ho, Moreno. What is this?"

"What's what?" Uncle Mike came over beside him.

"This was no bird."

"It had to be a bird."

"It was a rock."

"I told you," Uncle Mike said patiently, "there's no rock in the room."

"You looked?"

"Sure I looked."

"Did you look outside for a dead bird?"

"Yes."

"And did you find one?"

Uncle Mike paused. "No."

Mr. Straub shook his head, then began humming thoughtfully as he yanked off another board. "Well, we will put double plexiglass in the frames. That will not break."

"I really appreciate this."

"I like you, Moreno. You do good work. You smash the druggers."

"I'm hoping," said Uncle Mike, "that we all can bring them to justice."

"A baseball," Mr. Straub suddenly said. "Did you look for a baseball?"

"No baseball in the room either. And anyway, the window was broken after the game was over."

Mr. Straub frowned. "My daughter likes baseball. She loves the evils of the city. She needs to come back to the farm and get to work."

"Hey, Willy, she's not a bad girl."

"I know she is not a bad girl. But if she stays in town with all the boys and all the drugs, she will be."

"Hey, things will get better. Stick around for tonight's broadcast and you'll see."

Mr. Straub stared at the radio equipment. "Are you still talking on your radio?"

"Sure am. And tonight we're launching Belize Blockwatch."

Mr. Straub grunted. "I will get the plexiglass," he said, and left the room.

"Now you've done it, Uncle Mike," Rico said.

His uncle glanced at him. "What do you mean?"

"If Mr. Straub stays for the broadcast, Hannah can't play."

"Uh-oh. I didn't think of that." Uncle Mike glanced at the open doorway and lowered his voice. "But Willy needs to realize that we can't all just retreat to the country and hide on the farm. We've got to get involved."

*   *   *

"We've got to get involved," Uncle Mike repeated. It was broadcast time that evening, and he was at the radio controls. His theme song, "The Sound of Silence," was clashing faintly in his earphones. "Ready, Trent?"

The tall police officer who umpired the game sat beside Mike. He smiled a little tensely. "Ready."

"So you found a substitute ump?"

"For a couple of innings."

"Great. Ready, Rico and Justin?"

The boys nodded.

Down went Uncle Mike's finger. "Good evening, ladies and gentlemen. Welcome to tonight's broadcast, coming to you from the Way Station. Tonight," and he paused dramatically, "you may be listening to Belize's most important radio broadcast in a decade.

"Before we get to the game, I would like to introduce Officer Trent Morgan. His son Calvin is one of the star players for the Jaguars. I have the honor of being a member of his drug task force. And he's in support of a program we're calling Belize Blockwatch. Trent, tell us more." He swung the boom mike over in front of the officer.

The boys stood at the window. Justin's mind was split three ways. One part was watching the game, which had already started, so he could fill the listeners in once he got behind the microphone. Another part was listening to what Calvin's father was saying. But the third part of his mind was thinking *What happened to our window? Did someone down there break it? Am I looking at the culprit right now and don't know it?*

"Rico," he whispered.

"What?"

"Did Mr. Straub stay and watch?"

"I guess not," Rico said softly. "Hannah's playing."

"As you know, Mike," the policeman was saying, "Belize has a small police force. A lot of crime happens that we don't catch. That's where every person who's listening right now can make a difference. We need you to be eyes and the ears for the Belize Police Department. Communication is key. We have to stay in touch with each other. I have some suggestions for you. First of all—"

Suddenly he stopped, because Uncle Mike had grabbed him by the arm. "Just a second, Trent," Uncle Mike said. He took off the earphones and shook them, then grabbed for the silver radio and turned the tuning dial. "Testing, one, two," he said into the mike again and again. "Testing, testing, testing." His eyes scanned the meters and lights just once. Then he jumped up, ran to the window, and gave an ear-splitting whistle. Several people in the bleachers looked around. "Is the station coming through?" he roared.

"No, we can't hear you!" someone with a radio earplug in his ear shouted.

Uncle Mike heaved a huge, trembly sigh. "Well, that does it, guys. We're off the air."

CHAPTER 4

Mysterious Music

"Off the air?" Rico exclaimed. "But the power's still on."

"Yeah," Justin said, tapping the mike with his finger. "Look, the needles are still jumping."

"You're right," Uncle Mike agreed. "Everything's working here in the studio. But all of a sudden I couldn't hear us in the earphones, which I've got hooked to this big radio tuned to our FM frequency. We're generating a signal, but it's not even making it out to the bleachers." Suddenly he snapped his fingers. "The antenna. It's got to be the antenna."

He grabbed the earphones and clapped them on Rico's head. "Justin, you do play-by-play, and Rico, you listen. I'm going up on the roof to see what happened." He bounded out of the room. Officer Morgan hurried after him.

Justin took the mike, feeling a little foolish. "Hello, hello," he said. "Hear anything, Rico?"

Rico shook his head. "No, but keep talking."

"Turning now to our play-by-play,"Justin said, knowing he was talking just to himself, "let me give you a rundown of what's happened so far in the game. We're in the bottom of the second inning, and the Mayans are up. The Jaguars are ahead one to nothing, thanks to a home run by Calvin Morgan. Rico, hear anything?"

Rico shook his head, and rolled his hand in a "keep going" motion.

Upstairs there was a loud rattling on the roof tiles.

"Hannah Straub steps to the plate," Justin spoke into his dead microphone. "So far Hannah's one-for-one this evening. She hit a triple in the first, but had to wait on third while the Jaguar pitcher struck out the next three batters. Here's the pitch."

"I'm getting you!" Rico said suddenly, pressing the earphones tighter to his head.

"In the dirt for ball one," Justin reported.

"Now you've gone dead again," Rico said. "But keep talking."

"If I were the Jaguar pitcher," Justin continued, "I'd be very careful pitching to Hannah."

"You're coming through again!" Rico said. "You're really clear now."

"Because Hannah is deadly. She's got a really awesome eye, and if you throw it high and a little outside she'll nail it. Here's the pitch."

There was a tremendous crack, and Rico let out a shout. "Look at that!"

"Towering fly ball!" Justin shouted in an even louder voice. "She got under it a little, but it's 'way out there."

"Must be those farm-girl muscles," Rico said enthusiastically.

"You're not kidding. The right fielder Jason's got his eye on it. He dives! He's got it! No, he dropped it!"

"The setting sun was in his eyes," Rico suggested.

"Hannah's rounding second, on her way to third," Justin continued. "Rico, she's gotta be the fastest runner on either team. Here's Jason's throw. It's a bullet! Hannah's sliding! How she can slide in that dress, I don't know. Is she safe? Out? Safe?"

"Safe!" Rico said. "Her team is jumping up and down like a bunch of crazies!"

"I hope she gets a chance at starting that girls' softball—" Justin began, when a hand clamped over his mouth.

"Quiet!" Rico whispered in his ear. "Her dad might be listening."

Justin did the armpit thing with the mike, then whispered, "He can't hear all the way out at the farm."

Rico shrugged. "Whatever."

Officer Morgan suddenly appeared in the room. "Electrician's tape," he murmured to Rico. "Your uncle said there was some electrician's tape here somewhere. He's up there on the roof holding the wires together with his fingers." He and Rico began the search while Justin continued to broadcast.

A little while later Uncle Mike and Officer Morgan returned. A Mayan player had just struck out to end the inning. Uncle Mike took the headset and listened with one ear as he spoke into the mike.

"Well, folks, I hope you're enjoying the game," he said. "Sorry for the silence there. Something was wrong with the antenna. Trent, when our signal cut out you were just starting to give us some suggestions about how to make Belize Blockwatch work. Could you just pick up right there?"

"Sure," said Officer Morgan in his quiet voice, swiveling the microphone toward himself. Uncle Mike gave him the headset, and the policeman began to talk.

Meanwhile Uncle Mike beckoned the boys to the far end of the room. "Guys, look," he whispered. Reaching into his pocket, he removed a white cloth. "Ever seen this before?"

They stared at what looked like a piece of old T-shirt. Both boys shook their heads.

"When I got upstairs," the man said, "I found the antenna wire broken about six feet up on the pole. Snapped in half. And this cloth was tied to one of the broken parts."

A puzzled wrinkle creased Rico's forehead. "Tied to it?"

Uncle Mike nodded. "Now, I didn't tie it there, and you didn't tie it there. So who did?"

"And why?" Justin asked. "Do you think it caused the break?"

"It couldn't have. It's just a piece of cloth."

"What about the wire? Was it a clean break?"

Uncle Mike grinned. "Your dad's the detective, isn't he?"

"He used to be."

"The break was very clean. No rust, no signs of wear. Something had just snapped the wires."

"Or someone," Rico said.

"But we would have heard them," Justin protested. "Those tiles make a lot of noise. We would have heard them crunching across the roof toward the antenna, and we would have heard them escaping from the scene of the crime. But we didn't hear anybody on the roof until you went up there."

Uncle Mike's eyes narrowed thoughtfully. "Hmm, you're right. That means—" Suddenly he stopped. Officer Morgan seemed to be running out of things to say and was gazing appealingly at him. He took the microphone. "Thanks, Trent. We'll hear more from you later, but now back to the game."

Justin forced himself to concentrate on the action, even though Rico had taken over play-by-play duty. Calvin was up again and was taking ball after ball, waiting with his bat on his shoulder. Suddenly he swung gently and hit a soft grounder to third base. The third baseman, Philip Forrest, scooped it up, fired across to first, and got the jogging Calvin out by three paces.

"What's wrong with him?" Officer Morgan murmured. "Is he hurt?"

"Cal does that once in a while," Uncle Mike replied. "Hits a long one, then during the next at-bat he just seems to give it away. Is he just being nice to the other team?"

The policeman shook his head quickly. "No, Calvin doesn't play that way. He's a real competitor."

"That's what I always thought," Uncle Mike said.

"My son always has to be the best at everything he does," said Calvin's father. "No matter what sport he takes up, he competes hard."

"And does very well at whatever he tries," Uncle Mike added.

Officer Morgan sighed. "I just wish we could get a handle on this drug situation," he said. "I want a better Belize for my boy."

Rico suddenly placed the microphone under his armpit.

"Commercial break," he whispered.

"How," his uncle demanded in a low voice, "do you guys expect me to use that microphone after you put it in the places you do? Somebody get me a gas mask." He reached out for the microphone, waved it in the air a few times, then spoke into it. "Thanks, Rico. Folks, I hope you were taking notes when Officer Morgan spoke during the last inning break. We've got to keep in touch with each other. Communicate. Listen to the radio. Use the telephone. Kids, call your parents. If somebody sends you an e-mail, answer it."

Rico glanced around at Justin. "You got some more e-mail this morning," he whispered. "From both your folks and Monique."

"What did it say?"

"I don't read your e-mail."

"You can if you want to."

Rico snorted and stared out the window at the Jaguars, who in spite of Calvin's sloppiness were winning.

* * *

Later that night Rico wandered into the Way Station lobby, where this time Justin was watching Perry Mason all by himself.

"So who's Perry Mason?" he asked.

"Lawyer," Justin replied in a don't-bother-me voice.

"Must be a good one."

"Yeah."

"What does he do, go to court a lot?"

Justin crossed his legs. "Uh-huh."

Rico was silent for 15 seconds. Then he said, "You have nine e-mails."

"Thanks."

"The subject line on your dad's last message is 'From Your Lonely Papa.'"

Justin sighed and crossed his arms. "Rico, I'm watching this, OK? Just wait till I'm done."

Without a word Rico got up and left. But he was still awake when Justin made it up to their room. "I gotta say it, Justin. What's wrong?"

"What do you mean, what's wrong?"

"You."

"Me?"

Rico sat up in bed. "Yeah, you. You're losing touch."

"Hey. Just because I don't answer a couple of e-mails—"

"Nine."

"OK, nine. That doesn't mean I'm out of touch."

"And," Rico said, "I haven't seen you pray lately. Or read your Bible."

Justin almost said, "That's none of your business" but shortened it to "So?"

"I just thought I'd mention it," Rico said. His voice was low and steady, like it gets when a person argues about something with someone you don't usually argue with.

"Actually, Rico, what I do is my own business," Justin said in an icier tone.

"I know it is."

"Well, then—" Justin paused. "I'm going to bed."

"OK, go to bed."

"OK, I'll go to bed."

This conversation was followed by a lot of silence. Justin couldn't get to sleep, and by Rico's movements above him he could tell Rico wasn't asleep either.

Justin must have drifted off, though, because he suddenly jerked awake. It was totally dark. For a moment he wondered what had awakened him.

Then he heard it.

Soft, low music.

A radio, he thought. *Somebody's playing a radio.*

But the sound was moving. Not left to right, as it would be if somebody was carrying it along the hall. No, it was moving down to up. It had started very low, deep in the bowels of the old hotel. But now the sound had risen and was level with him.

Justin sat up.

The sound was in the wall. And it was still rising.

"Rico," he said softly.

No answer.

"Rico?"

The springs above him squeaked.

"Rico. Wake up."

"Huh?"

"Listen," Justin hissed. "What's that noise?"

There was silence above him for a while, and just as Justin thought his friend had gone to sleep he heard Rico take a deep breath.

"Music," Rico said. "A radio."

"Listen. Listen to where it's going."

"It's going upstairs."

"Rico, the stairs are in the other direction."

The springs jerked convulsively. "This place is haunted!"

Justin snorted. "Quiet. The music's coming back down."

The two boys listened as the music traveled down the wall and far below the floor, and finally they couldn't hear it anymore.

"Justin, what was it?"

"Sounded like a radio."

"Radios," Rico said in a quivery voice, "don't travel through walls. It moved."

"It was real music, Rico. You heard it, right?"

"I heard it. And I think we're staying in a haunted room. Somebody died in this room."

CHAPTER 5

A Notable Threat

As Justin lay there in the dark bedroom thinking about Rico's last comment, he was certain that he wouldn't get a lot of sleep that night. But he was wrong. And this time he had a dream that he was in his schoolroom and was signing autographs for his classmates, since in the dream he was a famous network baseball announcer. He signed autographs until suddenly a blinding light struck him full-force. It was sunshine coming through Willy Straub's new double-plexiglass windows. Staring up at the springs above him, Justin got the feeling that Rico wasn't there. He reached up and carefully pushed. Nothing.

"Rico?"

Rico shuffled through the doorway a minute or so later with a piece of paper in his hand. "Uncle Mike's gone," he said. "He left a note."

Suddenly Justin remembered the ghostly midnight music, and shuddered. "Where'd he go? When's he coming back?"

"Here's what he says." Rico tipped the paper toward the light. "'Guys, I'm out on an errand. Get showered and dressed as soon as you read this. Thought you might want to come down to the police station with me. Give you a chance to see some more of the town. We'll eat on the way.

Remind me to tell you the bad news about Hannah." It was signed "Uncle Mike."

"Whoa." Justin jumped out of bed and started gathering his shower supplies. "That's all he wrote?"

"Yeah. I wonder what happened to Hannah?"

Twenty minutes later Uncle Mike got back and told them to pile into the car.

"What happened to Hannah?" Rico asked as they drove through the tree-lined streets.

"Bad news," Uncle Mike said glumly. "Willy's taken her back to the farm with him."

"What?" both boys said in unison.

"It's true."

"For how long?" Rico asked.

"Why? What did she do?" Justin demanded. "And what does it have to do with the police?"

"Nothing to do with the police." Uncle Mike sighed. "She just hit a home run last night, that's all."

"Oh, no," Rico moaned. "So Mr. Straub was at the game after all. I didn't see him."

"No, Willy wasn't there."

"Then he heard it on the radio," Justin said. "But I thought you said he couldn't pick up your station on the farm."

"He didn't go back to the farm last night," Uncle Mike said gloomily. "He was staying with his sister, Nellie. She's the aunt Hannah's been helping in her Mennonite bakery. That's where we're eating this morning. When I called Nellie up to find out what time she opened, that's when she told me about Hannah."

Rico gave a low, mournful whistle. "So it *was* the broadcast?"

"You've got it," his uncle said. "Nellie is one of my faithful listeners, and she had the game on."

"But wait," Justin said. "Didn't Hannah hit the home run while the station was off the air?"

"No," Rico said, "it was just after we came back on the air. I heard you describe it in my earphones."

Uncle Mike chuckled ruefully. "And you must have really painted a wow of a word-picture, Justin," he said. "Nellie told me. All sorts of things about bullet throws and Hannah sliding into home and 'Is she out or is she safe?'"

Justin buried his face in his hands.

"Oh yeah," Uncle Mike continued, "you'll get the Broadcaster of the Year Award in Nellie's book." Uncle Mike chuckled some more, then reached over the seat to ruffle Justin's hair. "Hey, cheer up. You were just doing your job." He turned a corner. "Anyway, Willy's blood pressure zoomed off the charts and when Hannah got home he scolded her and ordered her to pack her suitcase right then and there."

Justin moaned.

Uncle Mike parked beside a line of storefronts. "You need to be very nice to Nellie this morning," he said to the boys. "She's not in a very happy mood."

Uncle Mike was right. Nellie, the usually warm-sounding blond woman behind the counter, gave them a narrow look when they entered the bakery. Justin avoided her gaze and looked around the bakery instead. Tall glass cases surrounded them, filled with rolls and brownies and giant crusty loaves of brown bread. The aroma was sheer delight.

"Good morning, Nellie," Uncle Mike said cheerfully. "We've got two growing boys here, so we're going to reduce a whole lot of your inventory. Brace yourself."

Out of the corner of his eye Justin saw Nellie move sideways, and he heard the metal clank of a walker move with her.

"What can I get for you?" she said. Her tone was chilly.

"You guys hunt around and find what you want," Uncle Mike told the boys. He went and leaned over the counter toward Nellie, and spoke in a voice just loud enough for Justin to hear. "Nellie, listen. I am sorry. The boys and I had no idea Willy was listening to the broadcast. We're so used to him being out on the farm all the time. We never suspected."

"I don't know what I'll do without her," Nellie said, a little less frostily. "I'd been hoping she'd get to stay all summer."

"Willy had better find a replacement," Uncle Mike said. "You really need someone now that you're using that walker."

"Willy said he'd send one of the nephews, but there's not a one of them who'd be as good as Hannah." She glared at Uncle Mike. "They'd probably spend all their time over by the Way Station playing ball. Here," she said suddenly, "try one of these brownies. Hannah baked them."

"Ohhhhh, Nellie, back away," Uncle Mike warned. "I'm not responsible for my actions when I get a brownie attack." He took a bite, and sighed. "Delicious as usual. Give me three more. Hannah's got the touch."

"And my fat-headed brother," she snapped, "is such a

beast about her baseball games. He might like living in the eighteenth century, but he shouldn't force her to, Mennonite culture or not. Well, you young broadcasters," she called across the room in what was by now an almost cheerful tone, "what can I get for you?"

*   *   *

One of Belize's short but heavy rainstorms pounded Uncle Mike's car as they drove from Nellie's bakery to the police station. Once they'd scurried inside, Uncle Mike paused. "You can wait here for me," he said, "or when it stops raining you can stroll around the city a bit. Stay on the main streets, and make sure you're back here at 11:00." He disappeared behind a door where a drug task force meeting was taking place.

"Guess what," Justin said to his friend. "We forgot to tell your uncle about the music last night."

Rico glanced quickly at him. "So that really happened?"

"Sure it happened."

"I got to thinking maybe I dreamed it. That was weird."

Suddenly they heard a clanking down at one end of the hall, and glanced in that direction. A tall boy was approaching them along the hallway, both hands gripping a mop handle. The mop was submerged in a bucket with rollers attached, and it squeaked as it came.

"Calvin, hi!" Rico said, waving his hand wildly.

The boy stopped and stared. Then his face broke into a cautious smile, and he continued moving toward them.

"Hello," he said. "I'm not sure—"

"I'm Rico, and this is Justin," Rico began, but Calvin's smile widened and he interrupted.

"You're the two who do the play-by-play for the games, aren't you?"

"Right," Justin said. "And we're glad we're not down on the field playing against you."

"I love baseball," Calvin said.

Rico glanced around. "This is where you work? Oh, that's right. Your dad is a police officer, isn't he?"

"Yes." A wistful note came into Calvin's voice. "It's about the only time I get to see him. Ever since he added this drug task force to his regular duties, he's the Invisible Dad." He sighed. "Sometimes I even send him an e-mail from home. He'll usually answer if he's in the office."

"E-mail is cool, isn't it?" Rico said in an expressionless voice, staring at the mop bucket.

"Justin's dad e-mails him from the U.S. He sends lots of e-mails."

"Nice," said Calvin politely.

"It's good when families stay in touch," Rico said thoughtfully.

Justin felt his face getting red. "So, Calvin," he asked, "what are your duties here?"

"I mop and do the lavatories and other stuff just about every day. Away from here I do other odd jobs too, and I'm banking the money I earn. I'd like to play ball in the United States."

Justin grinned. "Maybe someday we'll be trading your

baseball card."

Calvin smiled modestly. "As soon as I get a little older I'm going to see if there are any openings on teams in Puerto Rico or the Dominican Republic. If I can, I'll play in either country for a while. They say those are good places to catch the eye of the U.S. scouts."

After chatting for another minute, Calvin decided he'd better get back to work, and pushed off down the hall.

"Let's see if it's stopped raining," Justin said, glancing at his watch.

Rico headed for the door, opened it, and peeked cautiously at the sky. "Good, it's stopped. Now we'll be able to pick up lots of tourist things you can tell your dad about."

"Rico," Justin said in an annoyed voice as they began strolling down the street.

"It's getting pretty embarrassing," Rico continued, "when you won't answer the e-mail from your family."

"I'll get to it."

"Here." Rico suddenly reached into his back jeans pocket and brought out a folded wad of paper. "I printed them out for you. When we get tired we can sit down on a bench and you can read them."

Justin sighed, and stuffed the wad into the back zippered pocket of his backpack. "I just don't like to write," he said.

They walked up to Haulover Creek, and as they crossed the swing bridge onto Queen Street they could look out to the southwest to where the creek widened into the Caribbean Sea. A tourist pamphlet they bought told them that the city was 300 years old, and that the British had helped them defeat a Spanish attack in 1798. Most of the population, the pamphlet said, was made up of the descendants of the African slaves who in the late 1700s did the tough and dangerous work of logging.

It was all very fascinating, but not as fascinating as the strange events that had been happening at the Way Station.

*   *   *

There was no game that night, so for the evening broadcast Uncle Mike let the boys run the controls while he played the BBC news from his powerful short-wave radio. They also read over the air some news articles Uncle Mike had printed out from online newspapers around the world. Later Uncle Mike talked more about his Belize Blockwatch program.

"Don't forget," he said, "to come to the Blockwatch kickoff next Monday night. There'll be music and potluck food and all sorts of fun. And there will be a game between either the Mayans or the Jaguars and a team made up of police officers. Invite your friends and neighbors. And invite at least one family member to travel in from the country. Don't miss it."

Later, Rico finally convinced Justin to reply to his dad's e-mail. So Justin dashed off a couple of quick paragraphs. He told about doing the play-by-play for the games, and mentioned the broken window and snapped antenna wire. He talked about the players, including Calvin.

"Calvin and I have something in common," he wrote. "His dad is a police officer. I think he's on a drug task force or something."

Then he hurried down to the lobby to watch Perry Mason with Mary. When he finally came back upstairs, his eyes were stinging from watching the TV. The room was dark, but he could see Rico was asleep, his Bible at his side. Justin glanced at his own Bible, but rubbed his eyes and undressed for bed. His eyes were already closing as he lifted the covers and toppled onto the bunk.

"Ouch!"

"Wh-what?" said Rico in a surprisingly clear voice.

"Rico, this isn't funny."

Rico cleared his throat. "Justin? Is that you?"

"Of course it's me. How come you put a rock in my bed?"

The springs creaked. "I don't have rocks in my head."

"I said 'rock in my bed.' It's gotta be a rock. I just hit my head on it."

Rico said patiently but sleepily, "I didn't put a rock in your bed."

"Wait a minute." Justin felt around and seized the rock. "Hey, there's paper wrapped around it."

Suddenly the upper springs creaked and Rico's wide-awake face peered down. "A rock with paper around it?"

"Yeah." Justin strolled over and switched on the light, then unwrapped the paper. "There's writing on it."

"What's it say?"

Justin squinted through his stinging eyes. "Whoa."

Impatiently Rico snatched the paper. "'Stop the broadcasts,'" he read aloud, "'or someone will get hurt.'"

CHAPTER 6

Undercover Getaway

Rico jumped off the top bunk and darted over to where Justin was standing. When he saw that Justin was holding the paper delicately by its edges, he didn't touch it, but simply stared at it. The message had been written in black marker.

"How," Justin asked softly, "did that end up on my pillow?"

Rico shivered. "We were gone all day. Somebody could have come in."

"Remember that deadbolt lock? Nobody else could have come through that door." Justin scanned the room. "And anyway, there are only two ways anyone can get into the room. Through the door, and through—"

"—the window," they both said together. They rushed over to it.

"Locked from the inside," Justin said.

"And protected by two layers of Mr. Straub's plexiglass." Rico knocked on the layer closest to him. They stared at each other.

They stared at each other. Then Rico got his room key and they both slipped out into the hall, locking the door behind them. As always, Isaac's door was open.

Uncle Mike turned very pale when they showed him the rock and its message. "No joke, right?" he asked them

sternly. "I'm not in the mood for jokes."

"No joke," they both said.

"OK. Go get your blankets. All three of us are sleeping in here tonight. You can have my bed. I'm going down to the basement and get that folding army cot I never thought I'd use. I'm going to put it right in front of the door here."

* * *

After breakfast the next morning, Uncle Mike had another announcement. He made it in a low voice after carefully closing the kitchen door. "Pack your backpacks with everything you'll need for a few days," he said. "I'm getting you out of here."

The boys stared at him.

"I'm taking you to Willy Straub's farm for a couple of days," he said. "Safest place in Middle America. That godly Mennonite farmer owns six shotguns and knows how to use them. And remember: backpacks, but no suitcases. If somebody's watching the Way Station we don't want to tip them off that you're moving out."

"What about the game broadcasts?" Rico sputtered.

"I'll handle them for a bit," Uncle Mike said. "But I need to keep you guys safe while I figure out what's going on around here. Why would anybody be so against my broadcasts as to break my window, snap my antenna wire, and now sneak in and threaten my nephew and his buddy? And how," he growled, "did they sneak into the Way Station in the first place?"

"Can we have a half hour to do e-mail?" Rico asked. "If we don't know how long we'll be gone, we're going to have to let our families"—he glanced at Justin—"both our families know we won't be getting e-mail for awhile."

Uncle Mike thought a moment. "Good idea," he finally said. "Just make sure you delete any of this morning's sent mail from the hard drive after you've mailed it off. Who knows what these people are capable of? I'm going out to a pay phone, which should be secure, and call Trent." Justin spent most of the half hour writing an e-mail to his detective-turned-journalist dad, listing all the strange things that were happening. He sent off the e-mail, then deleted it from the "Sent Mail" section of the hard drive. Then he packed his backpack until it bulged.

"All set, guys?" Uncle Mike whispered once he'd entered the bedroom radio studio.

"Ready," Rico answered. He grabbed his backpack and was about to head for the door.

Uncle Mike stopped him. "Just a minute," he said. Grabbing both boys' backpacks, he stuffed them down into the "Hate Mail" trash can. "Now," he said, grinning, "you two guys are going to take out the trash."

Rico and Justin each grabbed a metal handle on the side of the can and struggled down the stairs with it. Just outside the front door, and out of view of any of the Way Station's windows, they removed the backpacks and set them nearby while they emptied the can in the dumpster. Uncle Mike drove the car close, and after wrestling the backpacks inside, they were on their way.

"Finally," Uncle Mike said as they headed out on Western Highway, "you'll get to see some country."

Rico said in a sour voice, "So you're going to drop us at the farm and come back?"

"Hey, I've gotta do the broadcast," his uncle responded calmly. "What's wrong? You'll be perfectly safe out there."

"I'm not so sure," Justin said.

Uncle Mike glanced over his shoulder, surprised. "Trust me. You'll be safe."

"Remember, Hannah's there too."

Uncle Mike threw back his head and laughed so heartily that he almost went off the road. "So that's it! You're worried about what Hannah's going to say because your broadcast of her home run made her dad haul her back home?"

"Yeah," both boys said in low voice.

"Hey, that'll work itself out. She knows it's not really your fault. Oh, one more thing."

Rico glanced at him apprehensively. "Now what?"

"Willy's going to put you to work. Chores and things like that. Great opportunity to give you a taste of agriculture."

"Thanks, Uncle Mike. Thanks a lot."

His uncle chuckled. "It'll be OK. I told him to go easy on you. I said you were soft."

"Soft?"

"Sure you're soft. I'll bet Hannah's got more muscle than you have."

"No way!" Rico howled, but when Uncle Mike wasn't looking, he bent his arm and felt his biceps. Justin did the same.

Then they stared out the windows at the beautiful Belize landscape. Rain clouds swept over once in a while, dumping heavy rain against the car's wildly whipping windshield wipers, but within a few minutes there would be bright sunshine again, and the wipers would start to squeak. A little later they passed a large house set up on stilts near the city of Belmopan.

"Whoa, look at that," Justin said, pointing.

The house was painted several different colors, and its windows had shutters. A dark green palm tree splashed its fronds over the roof toward the road. Crisscrossed in front of it were several long clotheslines, and every inch of those lines was covered with clothing.

"Laundry day," Uncle Mike said. "But they'll be lucky if the clothes get dry."

"Justin, do you wanna move down here?" Rico asked.

Justin shrugged. "The food's good," he said.

"Hey, what about ol' Uncle Mike here?" the man said, faking a sob.

The boys laughed at the voice he used.

Uncle Mike continued in a more serious voice. "I really love these people. Every time I get discouraged and think I'll go back to Los Angeles I get this lump in my throat, and I just can't tear myself away. And right over there is a perfect example."

The boys glanced in the direction of his nod. In front of a high cement-block building three girls were playing with stuffed animals.

"See that?" Uncle Mike said. "The Black girl is Creole—her ancestors were slaves almost 200 years ago. The girl who isn't quite as dark is Hispanic. And the third girl is Caucasian. That's sweet to see. If those kids can grow up with that same color-blind accepting attitude, then this culture can't help but get better."

A little less than an hour later the car began to wind its way into farmland. Soon two huge red barns and several smaller buildings loomed on the horizon.

"If my directions are right, this is the Straub farm," Uncle Mike said. "I've never actually been out to see it, but Willy brags about it every time he sees me. He thinks I'm getting soft too." As they drove along the road, black cows and a huge black bull stared thoughtfully at them from behind a tightly stretched barbed-wire fence.

"Wow!" Justin said. "Look at the huge tractors."

"Willy's got a right to brag," Uncle Mike said. "If it weren't for him and the other Mennonite farmers, Belize wouldn't have as much milk and eggs and chickens and a whole lot of beautiful handmade furniture."

He guided the car into the long driveway leading up to a large white farmhouse. "I suppose you guys will want to get in touch with Hannah first thing," he said thoughtfully.

"Not really," Rico said quickly.

"No rush," said Justin.

"You poor guys. Well, I think I see Willy's pickup down by the far barn."

Mr. Straub, it turned out, was high atop the barn nailing

new shingles on a section of roof. He waved energetically, crawled gingerly across to the point of the roof, and descended a long ladder.

"Welcome, welcome!" he said, offering a huge and slightly greasy hand for them to shake. "My new farm boys! Aha! We will put you right to work!"

Rico and Justin glanced warily at each other.

"Don't worry. It is easy. Just moving some boards. Then we have chapel and then we have supper. And early to bed. Rudolf! Get away!"

A huge black dog had bounded into the scene. After barking loudly a few times, he lunged at both boys' faces and licked them delightedly.

"Hannah, she is cleaning floors in the other barn," Mr. Straub said. "She will see you at chapel. You staying for supper, Moreno?"

"Thanks, but I can't. Got to do the broadcast. I'll drive over tomorrow again. If not, I'll call."

"Hah." Some of the sunshine departed from Mr. Straub's manner. "The broadcast. Yah. All right, boys, here is what you do."

The boards he'd talked about had been delivered from a lumberyard, and he wanted them stacked neatly inside the barn out of the rain. Soon the farmer was back on the barn roof again, and Uncle Mike's car was purring down the driveway.

"Think we're gonna get paid for this?" Rico asked his friend.

"I doubt it. Hannah probably doesn't get paid."

"Wonder where she's at."

Justin picked up another board. "He said over in that barn, cleaning floors. I hope she's working off her anger."

Rico shivered. "So do I."

As Justin worked, his shoulders grew sore. He glanced at his watch and wished someone had mentioned the time supper would be served.

"Rico," he said when there were four boards left. "Let's carry these all at once and get it over with. You get on that end."

"Cool."

They'd just bent down and lifted them halfway, when Rico suddenly dropped his end with a clatter to the ground. Justin howled with pain and dropped his end too.

"Rico," he yelped. "That hurt! What's your problem?"

But Rico had straightened up and was staring over Justin's shoulder with a strange, timid smile.

Justin turned.

Hannah was standing close behind him, her blue eyes boring into his. And he did not like the expression on her face.

CHAPTER 7

Stinky Business

"H-hi, Hannah," Justin said in a quavery voice.

"Hannah, great to see you," Rico said half-heartedly.

She stared at them stonily. Her mouth was tiny and very angry, and there were red spots on her cheeks. In each hand she held a pair of tall black rubber boots.

"Hannah, look," Rico began, "it wasn't our fault."

"I've got a job for you," she snapped. "Both of you."

"Uh, your dad asked us to move these boards," Justin said cautiously.

"And you're done with that, right?"

"Uh-huh. As soon as we get these last four in the barn."

"Well, get them in there."

Humbly, the boys hurried the boards into the barn, stacked them, and returned to Hannah, who was still standing in the same position.

"Put those boots on and follow me," she commanded, and began walking toward the other barn. The boys struggled into the boots, which were too big, and clumped after her.

"Uh, we like your farm," Rico commented to her back.

"Yeah, it's cool," Justin said.

"Way cool," Rico insisted.

She didn't say anything until they were standing in the

DSIB-3

other barn's doorway. An unpleasant smell wafted toward them, and both boys stepped back. Justin coughed a little.

"What's the matter?" she asked him.

"Ahemmm. Something in my throat."

"Have you guys ever cleaned barns before?"

Both boys shook their heads.

"Guess what," she said.

"We're going to get our chance now?" Justin asked timidly.

"You'd better believe it," she said grimly. "Grab that pitchfork. Rico, you take that other one. See that floor?"

"Yuck," Rico said. "I mean, yes."

"That floor is made of cement," she said. "But what's on top is manure. You know what manure is?"

Justin nodded. Suddenly an idea for lightening the moment struck him. "Say, Hannah," he said hesitantly, "this manure reminds me of a joke I heard. A city guy said to a farmer, 'Please tell me how long cows should be milked' and the farmer said, 'The same amount of time as short ones!' Get it? Long cows . . . short cows . . ."

Hannah glared at Justin. "As I was saying, the manure has got to be tossed onto that manure spreader over there," she said, jerking her thumb at a metal trailer attached to a tractor a few yards away. Apparently the trailer had been green at one time, but a lot of manure had stuck to its side and had rusted it.

Rico and Justin glanced at each other, then at the floor.

"All if it?" asked Justin.

"All of it," Hannah said. "And when you're done, I want to see cement." She started to walk away, and then turned back. "When you hear a bell, that's chapel. Leave your boots here and come to that little building next to the house." She stalked away.

"Whoa," Justin said as he watched her go. "She's mad."

"No kidding." Rico turned his gaze to the black, sticky muck on the barn floor. "Justin, I don't believe this. Where do we start?"

Justin shrugged. "We just start hacking, I guess."

So they hacked. The manure was thick and tough, so thick that it was like trying to tear up a carpet piece by piece—everything stuck to everything else.

Fifteen smelly minutes later they were still hacking. They'd managed to uncover a few small holes with cement at the bottom, but neither boy was making much progress.

"What do they feed these cows anyway?" Justin snarled. "Whatever it is, it's too . . . tight."

"I don't think cows did this; I think it was pigs."

"How do you know?"

Rico jerked his thumb toward the open doorway. "I saw some pigs in the pen outside. And I see little pig footprints in this muck." He rubbed the side of his nose with his finger. "How come you didn't spot those footprints? You're the detective."

Justin watched him. "Bad move."

"What do you mean, bad move?"

"You just got something on the side of your nose."

Rico looked alarmed. "What? What did I get on the—" He rubbed his nose, and then suddenly switched hands. "What was it? Is it gone?"

"Some of it."

"Get it off of me, quick," Rico begged. "Here, rub it off. With a clean hand," he added earnestly.

Someone burst into a girlish giggle behind them. They whirled. Hannah stood in the doorway, hugging herself, hooting in joyous laughter.

The boys watched her sternly until she finally calmed down.

"Is this all you've done?" she asked, trying to put on a stern face and voice.

"We've done the best we could," Justin said firmly.

"Oh, you guys," she sputtered. "You wouldn't last half a day on this farm. Here, give me that," she said, grabbing Justin's pitchfork. He could see that she had rubber boots on under her long dress.

"Look," she said, stabbing with the fork. "You've got to get under the edge of it like this. And then lift, to loosen it. Then tear forward." She tipped the fork handle up and there was a soggy tearing sound. "Then dig under the edge a little farther. Then tear forward."

The boys watched this lifting and tearing reverently. In just two minutes she'd cleared more manure than they'd cleared in a quarter of an hour.

"Now, try again," she said.

But suddenly a bell clanged in the distance.

"OK, boots off," she said. "Let's go."

Chapel took place in a large room with lots of windows and long wooden benches. Several farmhands, along with Mr. and Mrs. Straub and Hannah and the boys, sat on the benches while another farmhand stood behind a pulpit and read aloud in German from an old book. Then someone had a prayer, and everybody went to another large room for supper. The men ate first, and then left. Justin and Rico stayed behind waiting for Hannah. Finally she joined them, her hands red from washing pots and pans.

"How are you feeling?" she asked them in the kindest voice she'd used all day.

"Sore," Justin said.

"Smelly," Rico added.

"Sorry I was so snappish," Hannah said.

"That's OK," Rico said. "And we're sorry about getting you into trouble with that broadcast."

"That did hurt," she said.

"I know how much you like baseball," Justin told her.

She glanced quickly at him and shook her head. "That's only part of it. Baseball is fun, but it's Auntie I'm worried about. How is she going to run the bakery without me?"

"Did you tell your dad that?" Rico asked.

"Of course," she said glumly. "And he's sending one of my cousins to take my place. A guy. He's pretty useless. He can't give Auntie the kind of help she needs in the bakery. And he'd probably eat up all her products."

A loud whistle sounded from somewhere outside.

Hannah jumped up. "It's Father," she said quickly. "He's got something he wants me to do. Come and help."

Out in the yard they met an impatient Mr. Straub. "Hannah," he said, "you forgot to switch the sheep."

Hannah gasped. "Sorry."

"Go, go. Go!" He made shooing motions with his hands, and Hannah snatched up an empty metal pail and darted away.

"How," Justin panted as he and Rico ran along behind her, "do you 'switch sheep'?"

"Easy," she said. "I'll let you do it if you want. They've eaten down one pasture really low, and we need to move them to another one across the road."

"You're going to move a herd of sheep across a highway all by yourself?"

"No," she said. "You're going to help."

Rico swallowed. "Hey, look. I'll go clean more manure if you want. I never did anything with sheep before."

"You never did anything with manure before, and look how easy that was."

"Uh, yeah," Rico said doubtfully.

"Calm down," Hannah insisted. "It'll be fun."

She led them down the long driveway and out onto the main road. After leading them on a quarter-mile jog, she stopped at a gate. Justin could see a huge flock of white sheep far away in the pasture. He went to the barbed-wire fence and started to climb over.

"Where are you going?" Hannah asked, puzzled.

"To go herd the sheep," he said. "I thought—"

"Stay where you are." She removed a wire loop and swung the gate open. "Rico, you go down the road to that gate on the other side. When you get it open, wave, and then stay out of the way. Justin, you hold this pail."

Rico looked doubtfully at the distant sheep. None of

them was paying any attention to the three humans. Then he jogged down to the other gate, dragged it open, and waved to them.

"Rattle," Hannah said.

Justin shook the pail, which made a clanking sound.

"Sheep! Sheep! Sheep!" Hannah called.

For a few seconds, nothing happened.

"Rattle some more," Hannah said, and Justin rattled again.

Suddenly a distant sheep raised its head and looked alertly toward them. Justin gave another encouraging rattle. The sheep broke into a run, heading their way. Almost immediately all the other sheep looked up and started to run in their direction, leaping and bouncing. The thundering of little hooves filled the air, and the sheep got closer and closer.

Justin froze with fright.

"Move it, Justin," Hannah said calmly. "Follow me. Come on!" She raced down the road and Justin hurried after her. Behind him he could hear the sheep leaving the pasture and clattering madly along the gravel road behind them.

"Hurry, Justin!" Hannah panted. She darted through the gate. "In through here!" They ran about 30 yards into the pasture and Hannah shouted, "Drop the pail and run to the side!" Finally safe on the sidelines, Justin and Hannah and Rico watched the squirming sea of wool widen as the sheep poured through the gate into the pasture and surrounded the pail.

"That was incredible," Justin told her. "How did you train them to do that?"

Hannah looked thoughtful. "I don't think I ever trained them," she said. "They've known me since they were lambs. And I've always been the one to give them their dinner. When they were little I would always bring that pail with feed in it. I guess they got used to hearing the pail rattle, and they still come when they hear it."

She locked the gate securely, and together they started back along the road. "Listen," she said. "I need to talk to you about something."

Justin glanced at her. There was no longer a humorous twinkle in her blue eyes, and her face looked older and more serious than he'd ever seen it.

"Something is bothering me," she continued, "and I don't know what to do about it."

"We may not know a lot about farmwork," Rico said, "but we can listen."

She grinned at him briefly. "This isn't about farmwork. It's about—back there in Belize City. About the game."

"The broadcasts?"

"No, not the broadcasts." She paused, scuffing her leather work shoes in the gravel as she walked. "Look, I don't know how long this should be kept secret, but for now you've got to keep it quiet. OK?"

"Is it something illegal?" Justin said automatically. "Because if it is—"

"Justin's dad was a police officer," Rico explained.

"That's just the trouble," she said. "I don't know." She sighed. "But I'm going to go ahead and tell you. I want to see what you think about it."

"What's it about?" Justin asked.

She stared at him. "It's about Calvin. And what he might be mixed up in."

CHAPTER 8

Calvin Is a Milksop

The boys stared at her.

"What's Calvin been doing?" Rico asked.

"It's hard to explain," she said. "But it happens during the games. You know he's a pretty good player."

Justin nodded. "Just like you."

She gave him a half-smile. "And when we get out there on the field we do our best every time we get up to bat."

"Like your home runs," he said.

She stirred uneasily. "Let's not talk about my home runs right now, OK?"

"OK," Rico said quickly. "Go on. Don't interrupt her, Justin."

"The game starts. At Calvin's first at-bat he hits a homer or a triple. But at his second at-bat he turns into a milksop."

Justin blinked. "A what?"

"Milksop. Sissy. Wimp." She paused and shook her head. "I've been trying to figure out if I've been imagining things, but I don't think I have. On his second at-bat, Calvin doesn't swing away. He either bunts or sends a low grounder somewhere. And if he hits a fly, he never swings hard. It's more like he's swinging—carefully."

"I noticed that," Rico said.

Hannah looked at him eagerly. "You did? Justin, did you notice it too?"

"I think so."

"I know so," Rico said. "But I thought it was because Calvin was taking pity on the other team and giving them a chance."

Hannah quickly shook her head. "No. Calvin's too competitive. He'd never do that. There's some other reason he's holding back."

"But why would he do that?" Justin asked.

"I've got a theory," the girl replied.

The boys leaned forward.

"I think," Hannah whispered, "that he's signaling somebody."

Rico frowned. "Signaling somebody? Signaling who?"

"I don't know. That's what I'm trying to figure out. But I've noticed that he always waits for the right pitch. He'll let balls and strikes go by, just waiting for the one he wants."

"To do what?" Justin asked. "To aim it at somebody?"

"I think so. But it's not always the same person." By this time they were about to turn into the farmyard gate, so Hannah paused. "And there's something else that worries me too. Calvin has too much money."

"Uh-oh," Justin said.

"Drugs?" Rico whispered.

"I hope not." Hannah was on the edge of tears. "I really hope not."

"So how can you tell he has more money than he should?" Justin asked.

"His father is a police officer, and they don't make a lot. There's no mother in the picture. But he has a brand-new baseball glove. And then there's the second team book."

"What's a team book?" Rico asked.

"It's a booklet with all the players' pictures in it," she replied. "Your uncle spent a lot of time getting a bunch of businesses to buy advertising space in the first one. It was black and white. But Calvin wanted one in color, so now we have one. And there are only a few ads in it. So somebody paid out a lot of money."

"Calvin's got a job, you know," Justin said.

"His janitor job?" she said. "That doesn't pay enough to put out a team book in color."

"So," Rico said, "what do you think we ought to do?"

Justin interrupted. "Talk to Uncle Mike."

Hannah gave him an agonized look. There was a wrinkle between her eyebrows. "But what if I'm wrong? And what if I'm right?"

"He's the one who's wrong if he's dealing drugs."

"Funny thing," Rico said. "Calvin doesn't seem like that kind of guy."

"I know," Hannah agreed. "I don't want to get him into trouble, and I don't want to smear his name. I've been praying that I'll do the right thing."

"So will we," Rico said.

She glanced at him. "You pray?"

He nodded. "Justin does too."

The wrinkle between her eyebrows disappeared. "Oh, that's a relief," she sighed. "I was feeling so lonely in all this. I mean, I know that God is up there. And He's been so good to me."

They walked in silence for a moment until they came to the gateway to the farmyard. Rico got an embarrassed look on his face. "Hannah, where's the—restroom?"

"In the house," she said. "That's where you're staying."

"Thanks. See you later."

"Hannah," Justin said, "I've got a quick question."

"Sure. What?"

"How do *you* pray?"

Her eyebrows rose. "You mean, how does a person pray?"

"No, how do you pray?"

"Don't you know how?"

Justin glanced over his shoulder at the house. Rico had almost reached it. "Look. I'm the one who got Rico interested in being a Christian. A couple of months ago somebody stole something that belonged to his sister, and I helped Rico get acquainted with God."

"Chil-ly."

Justin paused. "Chilly?"

"I mean, cool. Isn't that the way you Yanks say it?"

He grinned. "Yeah, cool. Anyway, Rico got interested in reading the Bible and praying and all that kind of thing." He looked guiltily over his shoulder. "I think Rico knows how to pray better than I do."

"Are you sure?" she said doubtfully. "I just—pray. I don't try to figure out whether I'm doing it better than somebody else."

"OK, how do you do it?"

She gave him a blank look.

"I mean," Justin said, hoping the sunset was covering up how red his face was, "I know all about getting down on my knees and saying 'Dear Heavenly Father' or 'Dear Jesus' and all that. I know about confessing my sins and asking for forgiveness and praying for other people. I prayed for Rico a lot, I remember."

Hannah gently bit her lower lip. "So what you're wondering is—"

"—how to do it better," Justin finished desperately.

"Well, just talk," she said. "Just talk to Him about things you're interested in."

"Just talk?"

She nodded. "I mean, how do you talk to your parents? Like when your dad sends you an e-mail from the U.S. How do you write back? What do you say?"

Come on, sunset, cover me, Justin thought, as his face flamed even brighter. "Actually," he said, "I haven't been very homesick, so I've kind of been ignoring their e-mails up until just recently."

Hannah smiled. "I know how you feel a little bit. When I first went to town this summer I didn't feel really homesick. I was glad to get away from the farm and do something new for a change. Besides, I was with Aunt Nellie. I didn't even care whether Mother or Father called for a few days. But when I got to wondering about Calvin, that's when I got homesick. I can't talk to Father about it, of course. I wish I could; maybe someday I can. But I can talk to God."

The house door banged, and Justin glanced around. Rico was coming down the front steps. But he paused, and then went back in.

"So what do you do?" Justin asked quickly. "How do you pray?"

"Most of the time I write sort of a letter to God in a notebook," she said. "Every day, pretty early in the morning. And sometimes I'll just talk with Him, like I'm talking to you. I can't hear Him, of course. But He talks to me sometimes in my Bible. It's like those sheep—they know my voice because they've listened to it a lot. Reading the Bible is like listening to God's voice."

"Yeah," Justin said thoughtfully. "Thanks."

"You probably knew that already," Hannah said.

He nodded. "But it's working for you. I needed that."

She glanced at the sunset. "We'd better go in."

The Straub home was filled with gloriously polished wood furniture. Mrs. Straub was shorter than Hannah, and spoke more German than English. Her mashed potatoes and gravy and her pasta casserole and her warm apple pie made Justin think of his family. Only by rapid blinking could he keep tears of homesickness from his eyes. He wanted to go right to the phone and call Mom.

He was doing reverent surgery on the apple pie when the phone rang in the next room. He could hear Mrs. Straub answer it in German, but suddenly she got a surprised tone in her voice and switched to English. "Ah, Mr. Moreno. Yah, he is here. Yah, I will get him for you." She appeared in a doorway and waved the phone at Rico.

He glanced at his two friends. "Shall I tell about Calvin?" he asked in a low voice. Justin and Hannah looked at each other, then nodded.

According to Justin's watch, Rico was gone for 10 minutes, long enough for Mr. Straub, with many a hearty laugh, to tease Justin about how Hannah could clean barns better than Justin could. "Stay here for the summer," the man said. "You will learn many useful things. I will teach you how to make a bookcase. I will teach you," and he slammed his palm down on the glossy table, making the silverware rattle, "how to make this. A man who knows how to make a table is worth something in the world. No?"

Rico appeared in the doorway and beckoned to Justin, who got up and joined him. He and Rico put their left ears close together, their heads facing in opposite directions, and put the phone between them so they could both hear.

"Justin? Are you there?" came Uncle Mike's voice.

"Here," Justin said.

"Listen, I've been telling Rico that we've got to find some way of getting Hannah back here so we can confront Calvin. It sounds like he's in really deep trouble, and we've got to convince him to tell his dad about it. Trent's a great guy but he's too tied to his job, and Calvin doesn't always trust him. Listen," Uncle Mike said again, this time in a new and firmer voice, "let me talk to Willy. I think I can talk him around. He owes me. A couple of years ago I made friends with his nephew and got him into drug treatment."

The boys put down the phone and went to get a still-smiling Mr. Straub, who disappeared into the room where the phone was. Twenty minutes later he came back, no longer smiling.

"So, Hannah."

"Yes, Father?"

"You go tomorrow with the boys."

Her eyes widened in amazement.

"But only for a few days," he commanded. "Moreno will be here at nine o'clock tomorrow morning. You will do your chores before you go."

"Yes, Father."

"We'll help," Rico said earnestly.

Mr. Straub stared at him for several seconds, then a tiny grin tugged at his tightened lips. "Hannah will show you hard work one more time."

* * *

Next morning, when a cheerful Hannah banged on their door at 4:00, it was hard to tell who was more surprised— the boys, that they had to get up so early, or Hannah, who couldn't believe that they weren't already up and dressed. The night before, she'd given them some work clothes her cousins wore when they came, and once they were dressed she led them through the dark to a gigantic white cement-block building where cows stood in rows.

"No," Rico's voice quavered. "We're not going to milk cows. No."

"What's that?" Hannah asked him briskly. "Milk cows? Sure. I thought you liked cows, since you knew a joke about them." The girl went to a gray box on the wall and flicked switches. Motors began to hum. She made some adjustments on several pieces of gleaming stainless steel machinery, then attached black hoses to the undersides of several of the cows. The boys had just begun to watch this fascinating process when she called to them.

"Come here, guys. Meet Gretel."

A huge black-and-white cow with a distrustful expression stared moodily at them.

"Gretel hates the machines," Hannah said. "So we have to milk her by hand. Ready?"

"No," said both boys together.

"Come on," she said. "Here. Like this." Placing a stainless steel pail under the cow, she sat down on a wooden stool. Soon the pail was ringing with the squirts of milk. "Now you try it."

"Go ahead, Justin," Rico said politely.

Justin was even more generous. "No, you first."

Hannah volunteered Justin, and soon he was tugging with all his might. Gretel made a noise that sounded like the horn of an eighteen-wheel tractor-trailer, and shifted her position.

"Yowtch!" squealed Justin. "She stepped on my foot."

"You've got to do it right," Hannah said.

Somehow, though Justin never knew exactly how, they got the chores done by 7:00. Quick showers and Mrs. Straub's gigantic breakfast got them ready for Uncle Mike's arrival. And an hour and a half later they were back in Belize City, in the lobby of police headquarters.

"Wait in the car," Uncle Mike said. "I'll tell Calvin we're taking him to lunch. We'll go to Nellie's, in the little side room."

CHAPTER 9

Secret in the Wall

"He's smiling," Hannah said as Calvin jogged toward their car, which was parked in front of the police station. The boy was carrying a half-zipped black gym bag with him.

"Hi," he said cheerfully. "Got enough room for me and my bag? I brought it with me so I could go right to practice afterward."

Uncle Mike, who'd followed him out the door, got in and started the car.

"This is a real treat, Mr. Moreno," Calvin said. "Hello, Hannah! Glad you're back. Justin, Rico, hi."

"Hi," they said.

And nobody said much more until they pulled up in front of Nellie's bakery. It was Calvin who spoke again.

"Mind if I take this inside with me?" he asked, grabbing the gym bag. "I've got my good glove here, and I wouldn't want anyone to steal it from the car."

"Sure," Uncle Mike said.

Under Nellie's supervision they picked out various goodies and soon were seated at a table in the bakery's tiny side room. As he went in, Justin saw that the door had a "Reserved" sign on it.

"M'mmmm, good," Calvin said, sinking his teeth into a

warm buttered roll. Watching him, Justin thought, *I wonder how that's going to taste once we tell him why we're here.* He glanced at Calvin's gym bag on the floor.

For a while everyone enjoyed Nellie's goodies, but finally Uncle Mike cleared his throat. "Calvin, I've got some questions for you."

Calvin glanced at him, eyes still happy.

"Who are you trying to signal during your second at-bat in the games you play?"

Calvin's smile froze. He brought the unchewed half of the roll away from his mouth. "I beg your pardon?"

"We saw you, Calvin," Hannah said in a trembly voice. "You either bunt it or hit a grounder, always very carefully."

The boy's eyes flicked from face to face.

Don't bluff, Calvin, Justin prayed silently. *Dear Jesus, please don't let him bluff. We've got to get this thing settled.*

"And where," Uncle Mike asked gently, "are you getting all your money?"

Calvin swallowed. "Money?"

"For the new glove. For the new team book, in color."

"I'm working," Calvin replied. "I have a job."

"You're not making that much. Not by a long shot."

Calvin looked out the little square window with blue checker-pattern curtains. "I'd rather not say, if you don't mind."

Uncle Mike's voice lost a little of its gentleness. "Does your father know about what you're doing?"

Calvin nodded quickly.

"So if I went to Nellie's phone right now and asked him, he'd clear it up?"

"He's in Belmopan over the weekend teaching a police training seminar."

Uncle Mike shrugged. "I'll go track him down."

Calvin's eyes were small with fear. "No. Wait."

There was a long silence. The longer the silence got, the less Justin felt like looking at Calvin's face, so his eyes strayed to the boy's gym bag. The unzipped half was gaping, and he saw the black shine of a new baseball glove, along with an orange-brown loop of rubber or plastic tubing. *What's that?* he wondered.

"Is it drugs?" Uncle Mike finally asked.

Calvin shook his head quickly. "Oh, no. No. Nothing like that."

Uncle Mike frowned. "Not drugs?"

"No."

"Then why won't you tell us?"

"It's really—nobody else's business but mine."

"Oh yes, it is," Uncle Mike said firmly. "It's *my* business. It's *my* Way Station window. It's *my* FM antenna. It's *my* broadcast."

Is it my imagination, Justin wondered, *or did Calvin glance down at his gym bag right then?*

"Somebody is out to sabotage my broadcast," Uncle Mike growled, "and I want to know if it has anything to do with the signaling you've been doing."

Calvin stared down at his roll, which he had now laid down. Some of the butter was slithering off the brown crust and onto the shiny white plate.

"Please, Calvin," Hannah said softly.

Suddenly he slumped forward and put his elbows on the table. "All right. I'll tell you. But you can't tell anyone else."

"I can't promise that," Uncle Mike said. "If you—or the people you're signaling—are breaking the law, that's a matter for your dad. You know that."

Calvin glanced longingly at the window, and then at the door, and sighed. "All right," he said again. "Have you ever heard of myxoma?" He pronounced it "mixoma."

Uncle Mike blinked. "Myxoma? Never heard of it."

"There's a plant that grows out west in the jungle. I don't know the name of the plant, but myxoma is what they get from it."

"What who get from it?"

"I'm coming to that," the boy said. "You know all the Chinese people that are coming into Belize?"

Uncle Mike nodded. "There's a growing Asian population. Go on."

"Well, a lot of Asians like myxoma. They think it helps keep them young. The women take the powder and use it on their faces, and—"

"How does it get to be powder?" Uncle Mike said.

"Some Chinese men have a little factory in a house somewhere. They take the plant and make powder out of it."

Uncle Mike frowned again. "Why haven't I heard anything about this?"

"Because," Calvin said lamely, "myxoma isn't exactly legal in Belize yet. It's legal in Germany and just about all the other countries of the world, and in China too. But it's still not legal here. Isaac says—"

He stopped, and closed his mouth quickly.

"Isaac?" Uncle Mike said. "The Isaac at the Way Station?"

Calvin's eyes now filled with terror. He shook his head, again and again. "No, no, no," he moaned. "I didn't say anything. No."

"Get a grip," Uncle Mike said shortly. "You're saying that Isaac is involved in this myxoma scheme?"

Calvin was silent.

"Look, Calvin, your dad's going to find out about this sooner or later. If you tell us everything, we can help him understand your side of it."

Calvin put the fingertips of both his hands on his cheekbones. He was silent for several more seconds, then swallowed hard.

"All right," he said. "Here's how it works. Isaac has a copy of the team book. He knows all the players. He tells me which player to hit to on my second at-bat."

"And?"

"That's it."

Uncle Mike's frown deepened. "What do you mean, that's it?"

"I don't know any more," Calvin insisted. "Isaac told me that in a couple of months Parliament is going to vote on it, so everybody can come out in the open."

"But why signal?" Uncle Mike asked. "Signal who? And what are they supposed to do once they get the signal? It must have to do with the delivery of this stuff, but why on earth is there all the secrecy?"

Calvin shrugged. "That's all I know," he said.

Uncle Mike leaned back in his chair and thought for a long time. "Well," the man finally said, "a lot of this rings true. Every once in a while I hear about whole ethnic groups who want the juice from tiger spleens, or the root from an exotic plant, or all sorts of other things. Sometimes they're for religious use, and sometimes it's just plain old drugs that get you high. After all, there are a whole mess of people in the U.S. who want to get their hands on a weed called marijuana."

"But," Rico said, "is that any reason to sabotage your broadcasts?"

His uncle nodded. "Good point. Calvin, do you know why people would throw rocks through my window over this myxoma stuff?"

Calvin shook his head.

"Must be a lot of money in it, and they don't want traffic stopped," Uncle Mike decided.

"OK. Let's assume the myxoma story is true. We'll have to tell your dad."

"No, please!"

"Calvin, what you're doing is illegal. Even though you don't know a lot about it, you're mixed up with a bunch of people who want to keep things secret. And maybe it's the same bunch who want to do my station damage for some reason. And we've got to find out. Now, who's staying with you while your dad's gone?"

"I'm staying with another officer's family."

"OK. You don't have any baseball games this weekend, so there'll be no signaling going on. The next time you play will be Monday at the Belize Blockwatch kickoff. Will you have to signal anybody then?"

Calvin shrugged. "I don't know. Isaac tells me where to hit just before the game starts."

"All right. We'll just leave things the way they are for a while. I'll drive you home now. Watch out for yourself."

"OK," the boy said. He had a haunted look in his eyes.

* * *

The weekend was a busy one. Rico and Justin went to church together, and then Uncle Mike took them to a lot of different places—the Belize City Zoo, where they saw a baby jaguar, and then to the Mayan ruins at the Xunantunich (shoo-nan-too-nitch) site, featuring one of Belize's largest ancient pyramids.

And Justin got to see a lot more Perry Mason reruns.

"Mail call," Rico said in a chilly voice. It was late Sunday night, and he had drifted into the Way Station lobby where, as usual, Justin was sprawled on a couch, deeply engrossed in watching lawyer Perry Mason and his secretary Della Street solve another crime.

"What?"

"You got some e-mail," Rico said. "From your dad."

"Thanks," Justin said, not taking his eyes off the screen. Perry Mason was having a really tense conversation with a judge in a courtroom.

"Your dad says he loves you, by the way."

"What? Oh, thanks." Justin peered at his friend.

"Thanks. Leave the computer on. I'll send them a note."

"Yes, Your Honor," said Rico a little bitterly, as he turned to go. "Thank you, Your Honor. Oh, by the way. Just a warning."

"What?"

Rico lowered his voice. "Isaac's got his door open."

"He's always got his door open."

"That bugs me, though. I don't trust him."

Suddenly Uncle Mike poked his head into the lobby. "Guys," he said in a low voice, "I need to see you upstairs in five minutes."

Five minutes later Perry Mason's problems had still not been solved. In fact, they had gotten worse, and even the usually calm Della Street was saying that she didn't know what they were going to do next. It was hard for Justin to leave them alone in this crisis, but he tore himself away and joined Rico and his uncle in the broadcast room.

"Ah, there you are." Uncle Mike was standing beside the open door as Justin came through. "I need you two guys to help me. Good night, Isaac," he called across the hall. "Have a good sleep." Uncle Mike closed the door and spoke in a lower voice. "Justin, Rico. I want to do a remote broadcast tomorrow."

"What's a remote broadcast?" Rico asked.

"A broadcast that's away from here."

"How come?"

"Well, the Belize Blockwatch happens downtown, and that's where the Mayan-Jaguar All-Stars are going to play the police officers' team."

"You're going to broadcast that?" Justin asked. "Cool! But how?"

"I'm going to take the equipment with me. But"—and Uncle Mike glanced at the closed door—"I don't want Isaac to know about it."

"But he's always got his door open," Rico whispered. "How are we going to get the equipment out of our room?"

"Through the window?" Justin suggested.

"No," Uncle Mike said with a twinkle in his eye. "There's a third way."

Both boys stared at him. Rico said, "A third way into the room? A trapdoor?"

"No, not a trapdoor."

The boys glanced around, at the bunk beds, the broadcast equipment, the floor, the ceiling, the picture hanging on the wall.

"We give up," they said.

Uncle Mike put his finger to his lips and went over to the picture. Quietly he removed it, revealing a little door in the wall about two feet square.

"It's a dumbwaiter," he said.

CHAPTER 10

Coded Warning

"What," Rico whispered, "is a dumbwaiter?"

"The kind that spills soup on you," Justin suggested.

Rico dug him in the ribs. "Perry Mason must do stand-up comic on the side," he snorted.

Uncle Mike opened the little door.

"Two ropes," Rico said. "So we tie the equipment to one of them and let it down?"

"Better than that," his uncle said. "A dumbwaiter is like a miniature elevator. People don't ride in it, but things do. This one goes to the kitchen just below us and then to the basement. That's so you don't have to carry food up and down the stairs. Watch."

He pulled down on one of the ropes, and the other one went up. It ended in a knot at the top of a hollow wooden box, which rose into view. "We'll set the radio gear in here," he explained, "and send it down in sections. One of you will have to go downstairs and unload it."

"Wait a minute, Uncle Mike," Rico said. "This might explain something."

Justin gasped. "Rico, you're right!"

"What are you guys talking about?" Uncle Mike asked them.

Rico's eyes were shining. "A few nights ago," he said,

"Justin and I were trying to get to sleep, and suddenly we heard this music. It sounded like it was inside the wall, but it was going up and down."

Uncle Mike stared at them.

"It must have been a radio or something," Justin said, "on this dumbwaiter."

Uncle Mike's mouth split into a huge grin. "For a minute I thought you guys were going to spring still another mystery on me. You're right. That's just what happened. I have this little transistor radio I carry with me to catch local news. I'd carried it down to the basement. The dumbwaiter doesn't have a door down there, so the shaft is always open. I set the radio on the shelf here, and then put some canned food on the dumbwaiter and hoisted it upstairs. Then I went up to the kitchen and discovered I'd sent the dumbwaiter up too high and had to pull it down again."

The boys looked at each other. "We thought this place was haunted," Justin said.

"Sorry to give you a scare."

"That's OK," Rico said. "Justin and I had been having an argument, and we weren't exactly talking to each other. That music in the wall sort of broke the ice."

"Look, guys," Uncle Mike said, "most any talk is better than no talk. Communication is good."

"I know," Justin said thoughtfully. "I found that out."

"But there's a time for action too," the man continued. "And that time is now. We've got to get this radio equipment downstairs. And Isaac mustn't learn about it. Justin, do you know where the basement door is? Good. The light switch is at the top of the steps. Just go down them, and you'll see the open dumbwaiter shaft. When you're down there, don't talk. We'll wiggle the rope to know when to start pulling. When the box comes down, just unload it and wiggle the rope, and we'll haul it back up."

Justin went to the door, walked casually through it, waved to Isaac (who smiled and waved back) and bounded down the stairs two at a time. On the first floor he softened his footsteps, and noiselessly opened the basement door only as wide as needed to get his body through, felt for the light switch, and descended the stairway. When he got to the dumbwaiter shaft, he waited. A minute or so later the rope wiggled and he started to pull. Soon the box arrived, loaded with equipment. He carefully stacked it all on the floor, then wiggled the rope. A couple of loads later the box arrived with nothing in it but a note.

"Good job," it said. "Put this note in your pocket, tiptoe upstairs, and watch another half hour of Perry Mason. That should keep Isaac from getting suspicious."

But even though Perry and Della's problems were tenser than ever, Justin barely got a grip on the plot. He was thinking about tomorrow, and Calvin, and the remote broadcast. And the mysterious myxoma, and why people would be trying to sabotage Uncle Mike's radio station.

When he got upstairs again, Rico was in bed reading his Bible. He took a piece of paper from its pages and handed it to Justin. "Uncle Mike went downstairs after we got everything sent downstairs," he said. "Then he sent me back this note."

"All the equipment's packed in the car trunk," the note read, "so we're ready for tomorrow night. Isaac's clueless, as far as I can tell. Rico, make sure the batteries in your Walkman are fresh—we might need it to check if we're on the air. Justin, once you see this note, tear it into tiny pieces and put it in the Hate Mail can. Lock the door, and get a good night's sleep, because you'll probably need it."

*   *   *

"Good evening, ladies and gentlemen, and welcome to our special remote broadcast from the Belize Block-watch kickoff."

Seated behind the wheel of his car, which was parked along the first-base side of one of the town's playing fields about a mile from the Way Station, Uncle Mike was wearing a hat with a wide brim. It was tipped down over his eyes, partly disguising him and partly hiding the microphone he held in his left hand.

Rico sat in the front seat on the passenger side with a sheet of paper on his knee and Walkman wires in his ears. He gave the thumbs-up sign and mouthed the words "Sounds good." "I want to thank you all for listening this evening," his uncle said, "but what I'd really prefer is that you turn off your radios—or bring them along with you if you have batteries—and join us down here at the corner of St. George and Sargeant at the Blockwatch kickoff. We've already heard from several of our excellent Belize bands, and Officer Trent Morgan will be along in a while to give you a bit of the fine speech he made a few moments ago, telling you how you can help be the eyes and ears of the Belize Police Department."

Justin stood on the other side of the car, glancing through the window into the back seat, where the two main broadcasting units glowed. A thick cord and a thin wire emerged from the car door and trailed away across the grass behind. Justin studied the jumping needles for a moment, then reached in and delicately adjusted a knob.

"It won't be long before the baseball action starts," Uncle Mike reported, "so let me give the microphone to my nephew Rico. Rico, tell us about the lineups for tonight's game."

"It's going to be different than usual," Rico said. "A team of Belize police officers are going to be playing a team of all-stars from the Mayans and Jaguars."

"Wait a minute," said Uncle Mike. "That doesn't seem fair. Aren't the grown-ups going to stomp the kids?"

"It actually should be pretty even," Rico replied. "The grown-ups will be stronger, but I've learned that several of them have never played even softball, let alone baseball. So we'll see what happens."

"How were the all-stars chosen?"

"The teams each voted six of their players to the all-stars. That gives nine regular players plus three substitutes if they need them. One interesting thing is that both girl players are on the list, one from the Jaguars and one from the Mayans. Another item of note is that Calvin Morgan will be playing against his own father. Now, here are the lineups. Batting first for the police team . . ."

While Rico talked, Uncle Mike motioned Justin to come around to the driver's side of the car.

"Hannah's playing?" Justin asked him in a low voice. "How did that happen?"

"I twisted Willy's arm. Hard," Uncle Mike chuckled.

"What did you say to him?"

"Look over there." Uncle Mike pointed. "See that big delivery pushcart with the huge wheels and the cover on top? Notice what it says on the side?"

" 'Nellie's Bakery.' "

"That's the cart Hannah's been using to deliver Nellie's bread to Belize City stores all summer," Uncle Mike said. "Hannah rolled a load of pastries down here this afternoon. I told Willy that it would be good advertising for his sister's business if Hannah played on the team tonight. He growled a lot, but he finally said yes. What's neat is that even before the game, Hannah's run out of goodies. That young lady knows how to sell."

"That's great!" said Justin. "Did you hear if Calvin got any word from Isaac about doing a signal?"

Uncle Mike shook his head. "I didn't hear one way or the other. It would be pretty daring with all these cops close by."

"But the myxoma people don't know we know anything. Did you tell Officer Morgan?"

Uncle Mike winced like he was in pain. "No. I took a chance and decided to wait until after today's events. If the myxoma story is true and it's just some antiaging potion, it's not that big of a deal. Say, why don't you stay out in the bleachers during the first part of the game and keep your eyes open? See if you can spot someone responding to a signal."

"OK." Justin started to walk away, but Uncle Mike called him back.

"Snack sack," he said, holding out a large paper bag. "Don't want you to forget that."

"Thanks," Justin said gratefully.

He carried the paper bag to the bleachers and squeezed in between two men. *It's nice to relax a bit,* he thought, placing the bag on the ground under the wooden seat. *A baseball broadcaster's life isn't for me.*

The man on his left had a small transistor radio, and Justin could hear Rico's tiny, solemn voice filling time. "The police are not wearing their regular uniforms tonight," Rico said. "Most of them are in T-shirts and jeans."

"It's going to be interesting," Uncle Mike's voice broke in, "to see how all the cricket players deal with the baseball bats. The two are handled totally different."

Finally the game started, and right away it turned into almost more of a comedy than a real contest. The police officers were up first, and most of them didn't even know how to stand at the plate, so they took a lot of ribbing from the crowd. They also swung fiercely at every pitch, so there were a lot of strikeouts. Three outs later everybody was expecting the all-stars to do a lot better, but it turned out that the police officers' pitcher didn't know how to hit the strike zone.

"The all-stars haven't had much to hit all inning," said

Rico's transistorized voice. "But now Calvin Morgan steps to the plate. I don't know whether he'll find the pitch he wants or—wow! He reached way outside for that one, but he got it! It's a high, towering drive to left field, out over the street. Uh-oh! It banged the top of someone's car out there. I hope it didn't do a lot of damage. An easy home run for Calvin."

His home run seemed to break the ice, and the all-stars started scoring so many runs that by the time their half of the second inning came around, Calvin was at the plate again. Justin slipped off the bleachers and headed to Uncle Mike's car, keeping a careful eye on Calvin. *I'm gonna make sure Rico doesn't tip someone off by the way he broadcasts this at-bat,* he thought. He'd just reached the car, where Rico was now kneeling on the front seat.

"Calvin swings," Rico was saying, "and it's a shot directly at the shortstop."

"Did you see that?" Uncle Mike broke in excitedly. "Talk about beginner's luck! The shortstop—who has never played shortstop in his life—just lifted his glove in self-defense, and the ball caught in the webbing!"

The crowd cheered wildly, and the dazed shortstop waved back at them.

"Justin," Uncle Mike said quietly, "keep your eyes open. If you see anything unusual, let me know."

Justin scanned the bleachers. The crowd was buzzing about the amazing catch. Two screaming teenage girls chased each other along the front of the bleachers. *Showing off to those four teenage guy teens sitting on their bikes,* Justin decided.

In the car Rico mouthed the words "I'm hungry."

Uncle Mike turned to Justin. "Rico's starving. Got the snack sack?"

"Uh-oh. I left it under the bleachers."

"Better go grab it."

Justin threaded his way through the spectators back to where he'd been sitting. Rather than disturb people he ducked under the rear of the bleachers, and soon was back at the car. He set the bag on the car's roof, got out a sack of potato chips, and tore it open for his friend. Then he took over the play-by-play. The all-stars were pulling so far ahead that it was getting to be a laugher. Experience was winning over strength, and the crowd was loving it, cheering the kids and jeering good-naturedly at the police officers' team. In the later innings the cops managed to tack on a few runs to soothe their pride, but at the end of the ninth, the all-stars had beaten them 10-6.

"Nice job with the broadcast, guys," Uncle Mike whispered to Rico and Justin while someone he was interviewing had the mike and was answering a question. "I'll probably be here for another hour or two doing interviews. Want to stick around?"

The boys glanced at each other. "I think we'll walk home," Rico said.

"Do you mind keeping an ear on the broadcast? This is the first remote I've done, and I'd like to get your feedback about the quality."

"Sure." Rico adjusted the volume on his Walkman. "'Bye."

Justin tucked the snack sack under his arm and to-

gether they threaded their way through the crowds and down the street. "This is heavy," he said. "Your uncle sure gave us a lot of goodies."

"I guess he thinks we're growing boys."

They'd gone about five blocks when Rico suddenly grabbed Justin's arm, hard.

"Ouch! What's wrong?" Justin asked.

"Listen." Rico yanked one of his Walkman earphones out of his ear and gave it to Justin. "Listen."

"—a little message for you," Uncle Mike was saying. "So Rico, I know you're listening to this broadcast, and I wanted to let you know that there are some teenage boys looking for Justin."

Justin could hear rising tension in the older man's tone. "They asked where you were, and I said I really didn't know. So Rico, if you're listening to this, I just wanted you to know they were looking for Justin. And they're on bicycles—"

The man's voice gave one hiccupy tremble and then steadied. "So keep an eye out, guy. Keep an eye out. And now I'm going to point the mike in the direction of this great marimba band that has just started playing."

The mellow marimba sounds filled Justin's ear, but in the distance he could hear Uncle Mike shouting, "Trent Morgan. Somebody get me Officer Morgan! I need to talk to Officer Morgan right now!"

CHAPTER 11

On the Run

"Come on!" Rico grabbed Justin's arm again. "We've gotta hide!"

"Why do these guys want to find us? I can't figure—"

"Figure it out while we're hiding." Rico started toward a shed in someone's backyard.

"Stop."

"Come on, Justin."

"No, look. If this has anything to do with the radio station sabotage, these guys will know we're connected to the Way Station. They know we'd walk there by the shortest route—and this is it. So they'll come this way and they'll search everything on the way. So you and I need to run sideways, at right angles, and keep under cover."

"Well, don't just stand here babbling, professor," Rico insisted. "Let's do it."

They dashed down a small side street for a block and a half.

"Here. Stop here," gasped Justin, getting behind a tree and pressing close to it.

Rico joined him. "Why?"

"For one thing, this snack bag is heavy. And for another thing, if we don't know where they are, they're more likely to find us. Let's wait here and see if we spot some guys with bikes go by back there."

Anxiously they stared back the way they'd come.

"There," Rico said. "One guy on a bike. Two. Three. Four!" he yelped. "Give me a break!"

"And they're all heading toward the Way Station," Justin said. "There were four guys hanging out together at the game."

"How do we know they're the ones who are after us?"

"We don't," Justin replied, "but it's probably them. Everybody else is down at the kickoff."

"Why do you think they're chasing us?"

Justin shook his head. "I don't know. Maybe they're trying to kidnap us to use us as hostages. Let's keep going down this side street."

"Let's stay on the lawns," Rico said as he started jogging, "out of view."

"Good thinking," his friend said. "Because pretty soon they're going to get suspicious and start hunting the side streets. And they've got bikes."

The boys darted along in silence for a while, feeling the soft grass underfoot, pausing at intersections and looking all four ways before continuing.

"Do you know where we are?" Justin asked.

"No."

They were crossing still another lawn when suddenly a dog's vicious snarl sounded close to them, and they dashed for the street again.

"We've got to get to the Way Station," Justin panted.

"If they're smart, they've staked it out." Rico gave a frustrated growl. "What do we have that they want? A bag of snacks? Hey, give me some more of those chips."

"You ate all the chips."

"Well, give me something else then."

Justin set down the bag, got down on one knee, and felt around inside. "Something's been rattling around in here," he said, "and I've been wondering if it's—"

He stopped. His hand emerged, holding a box of matches. "Hey. This isn't a snack."

"Well, keep digging," Rico said impatiently.

"Neither is this." Out came Justin's hand again, this time with a package of cigarettes.

"Uncle Mike doesn't smoke," Rico said in a puzzled voice. "Maybe Isaac asked him to get some."

Justin turned the bag over on the grass. Out tumbled a huge slab of cheese sealed in plastic, another pack of cigarettes, a large sausage, a box of dishwashing soap, and a bottle of Marie Sharp's hot sauce.

"This," he said in a dazed voice, "is not a bag of snacks."

"You got the wrong sack," Rico said. "How? What happened?"

Justin told him how he'd set Uncle Mike's sack under the bleachers. "And I remember," he said, "that when I came back for it, it was the only bag in sight. So I thought it was mine."

A dog barked in the distance.

Rico glanced up. "The bikes could be along any minute."

"Help me get this stuff back in here," Justin said

quickly. "Let's hide somewhere and figure this out. Is your uncle still broadcasting?"

"Yeah."

"Heard anything that might apply to us?"

Rico plopped the Marie Sharp bottle on top of the other stuff in the bag. "No. He's talking to a woman whose son is a gang member. She's saying how great a block-watch will be."

They found a little shed at the side of a vacant lot. It wasn't locked, so they slipped inside.

"You know what?" Justin said. "Let's just sit here and listen to your uncle."

"I'm listening to him."

"Let me listen too."

"Sure, if you want to," Rico said.

"Because he's really worried about us, right? Isn't he?"

"Right."

"So if he's worried," Justin reasoned, "he's not going to forget about us. He's going to try to stay in touch."

"Like your dad."

Justin glanced at him. "I know. Like my dad. Don't rub it in."

"And like God," Rico reminded him.

"Right." Justin grinned ruefully. "Like God." He reached out his hand. "Let me listen."

Rico handed him one of the earphones.

"—and good luck," Uncle Mike said in a cheerful voice, but Justin could tell there was tension in it too. "Our block-watch program should do a lot to help your son get the support he needs. We're almost ready to wrap up here," he said. "Just a minute. Hannah! Hannah, could you come here for a minute?"

There was a pause and a confused mumble of voices.

"Over here, Hannah," Uncle Mike called out. "I'm glad I caught you before you left. Ladies and gentlemen, Hannah Straub was not only one of the all-star baseball players this evening, but she's vice president of Nellie's Bakery here in town."

There was a giggle. "I'm not vice president."

"Or at least sales manager."

"I just work there," she said.

"What do you mean, just? Tell me about your big cart there. Is it heavy?"

"It's nice and sturdy. It has big wheels, and that's what makes it easy to push along the street."

"And you came down here with lots of Nellie's pastries, right? How did you do?"

"They're all gone."

Uncle Mike whistled. "Tremendous. Nellie, if you're listening, I command you to make your niece vice president right away. This girl is going places. So you're rolling this back to Nellie's now, right?"

"That's right."

"Keep an eye out for my nephew and his friend, will you? Tell them hi. That's sure a big cart. And totally empty, I think you said."

Rico punched Justin in the arm. "Hear that?"

"I heard it. He's hinting that we find Hannah."

"And hide in her cart," Rico said. "Let's go."

Justin paused. "Just a minute. I want to check something." He opened the door of the shed to let in some light. One by one he took the items out of the bag and checked them. "These are ordinary matches. This sausage looks real, but we'll put that on hold. Same with the cheese. The cigarettes are still sealed, though that might not mean anything." He shook the box of dishwashing soap. "This is sealed too. And so is this hot sauce."

He shook the bottle vigorously, and a funny expression came over his face.

"Let me see it," Rico said.

"Shake it."

Rico took the bottle and jiggled it energetically. "Feels funny."

"It feels like this box of soap."

"You're right. I don't think it's hot sauce in there. It's something else. Open it up."

Justin gripped the cap in his right fist and turned it hard. It finally came loose, and he pulled it off the bottle along with the shrink-wrap seal. Carefully he tipped the bottle into his palm.

"White powder," he whispered.

"Myxoma," Rico said.

"Myxoma, or something else. Now we know what they're after. We've got to get this to the authorities so they can find out for sure. Now," Justin said, screwing the cap tightly back onto the bottle and getting to his feet, "let's go find Hannah."

The two boys slipped carefully out of the shed.

"This is gonna be tough," Rico whispered. "For one thing, we don't know where her aunt's bakery is from here. For another thing, there are all these bicycles we have to watch out for."

"And," Justin said, "Hannah's a moving target. Look, let's do it like this. As we walk, you watch the front and the right. I'll watch left and behind. That way neither of us has to get neck whiplash."

"Bikes!" yelped Rico, and he and Justin dived behind a low hedge. To Justin's horror, the roots and lower branches of the hedge were pretty skimpy. But they lay there, absolutely still, praying that the people who owned that yard weren't home, praying that the bikers wouldn't look down and see them, praying that they'd find Hannah soon.

The bike came close, chains rattling. One of the wheels thwacked against the street like the rider had been doing a wheelie. One of the teens screamed at the top of his voice, "We know where you are, and we see you!" But they passed on by.

Rico and Justin lay low for about four minutes, just to be safe.

"Guess what?" Justin said. "Two of them had earphones on."

Rico gulped. "If they were listening to Uncle Mike, I hope they didn't pick up the Hannah hint."

Block after dangerous block they traveled, walking as casually as they could down the streets, but slowing at the intersections, their eyes darting all four ways, looking for bikes and Hannah's bakery cart.

Once they spotted one of the bikers alone, and hit the grass, flat. "Bad news," Justin said.

"They're splitting up. I guess that way, if one of them spots us, he can signal the others to come and help him."

Rico's voice was small and worried. "So what do we do if they catch us?" he asked. "Give them the powder?"

Justin paused. "We may have to give it to them. But if this is drugs and not just myxoma, these guys are gonna be a whole lot more dangerous. They might not want to let us get away."

"So like I said, 'What do we do if they catch us?'"

Justin stared at him without blinking. "We don't let them catch us."

Three blocks later they finally spotted Hannah, far off in the distance, pushing her cart in the opposite direction.

"It's probably half a mile," Rico said. "Let's just run for it."

Abandoning caution, they put down their heads and ran, pumping past intersection after intersection. Once they caught a glimpse of a single biker, but there was no alarm. But when they were two blocks from Hannah, a distant whistle split the air.

As the boys pounded toward the cart, the girl turned, and smiled. "Hi," she said. "Where did you two come from?"

"Hide us!" yelped Rico, clawing at the tough black plastic lid of her cart.

Justin glanced fearfully behind him. "We're being chased," he said quickly. "By dangerous guys."

"Hurry. Please help us!" Rico begged.

In an instant she had the lid off, and they tumbled up over the top. "What's going on?" she asked.

"Don't talk!" Justin hissed.

"Just push!" Rico urged.

She fitted the lid back into place, and her voice became muffled. "I can't push you two guys," she said.

"You've got to," Justin called to her desperately. "If the bikers see you just standing here, they'll suspect something for sure."

"Why are they chasing you?"

"Because," Justin said, "they want the cocaine we're carrying. And they probably want us too, to keep us from testifying against them. Please, Hannah, try!"

The cart tipped a little, and scraped along the sidewalk.

"I can't," she said. "This is a bakery cart. And you two guys weigh a ton."

"Know something, Hannah?" Rico asked her.

"What?"

"You'd never last a day on a farm."

There was a short pause, then a powerful jerk, and the cart began to move steadily along.

Inside, half-sitting on Rico, Justin sighed with relief. "Now," he said, "if she can just get us to Nellie's Bakery, we'll—"

Suddenly the cart stopped. He heard the skidding of a set of bicycle tires. Two sets. Then more.

"Hoy, there," a deep teenage male voice said. "What's in the cart?"

CHAPTER 12

Marie Sharp Steps In

"What do we do?" Rico whispered in the darkness.

"Struggle and run," Justin whispered back.

"Stop it," they heard Hannah say. "Leave my cart alone."

"Get back," one of the teens said. "How do you get the lid off?"

Hannah screamed, loudly. Her second scream was cut off halfway through.

Justin lunged up and popped the lid off, and Rico scrambled up beside him. In the sunset light Justin saw that one of the teens was holding Hannah and had his hand over her mouth. The teen suddenly yelped. "She bit me!"

One of the other teens lunged at the cart and tipped it sideways. It fell heavily, and Rico and Justin tumbled out. Hannah screamed again.

"Give me the bottle," one of the teens said to Rico. He clicked open a bright, wicked-looking knife. Justin's skin went cold and crawly.

Rico slowly crawled to the opening of the cart and reached inside. And as he did, there was a deafening siren-howl, and a police car whined around a corner and squealed to a stop. A loudspeaker crackled, "Put your hands up! Stay where you are!" Two car doors *thunked,* and suddenly Officer Morgan and Uncle Mike were beside them.

*   *   *

"So it was *cocaine?*" Rico asked.

It was late that night, and he and Justin and Hannah and Uncle Mike had just arrived at the Way Station's cozy kitchen from the Belize Police Department headquarters, where the other teens had been booked for harassment and assault with deadly weapons. A squad car had been sent to the Way Station, and Isaac had been taken into custody.

Using a blender, Uncle Mike had blended them a fruit drink that included frozen bananas, and they sat around the table sipping on it.

"Cocaine it was," he said. "The best high-grade, passing through from Colombia, on its way to the good old U.S.A."

"So the myxoma story was just a cover," Justin said.

Uncle Mike chuckled in an embarrassed way. "I'm an idiot for swallowing that line," he said, "and Trent told me so. He said, 'Why didn't you just look up myxoma in the dictionary?' He had one in his office, and we found out that it's a benign tumor. It has nothing to do with being a medicinal root."

"So this whole thing was a drug operation," Rico said. "And Isaac was involved in it?"

Hannah said, "And Calvin, too."

"Isaac, yes," Uncle Mike corrected her, "but Calvin, no. Calvin just thought it was myxoma. Or if he suspected it was something more, he never looked into it. He just collected

his hundred dollars a game and didn't ask questions."

Justin's jaw dropped. "A hundred a game? That should have told him something."

"I know. But he wanted so badly to save up enough to travel to a baseball country such as the Dominican Republic."

Hannah asked, "How did the operation work?"

Uncle Mike refilled their glasses. "Drug-smuggling operation. Cocaine arrived in southern Belize from Colombia. The powder was placed into clean Marie Sharp's hot sauce bottles, and capped and sealed, just like from the factory. The Marie Sharp company is going to be shocked and very angry when it hears how its empties were used."

"That's terrible," Hannah said. "Everybody loves Marie's sauce. But how did the baseball game come into it?"

"The police know that Belize is a route for drugs," he replied, "and they suspected a lot of the smugglers already, but it's been hard to get proof. So the smugglers needed some way to get the powder from point A to point B without anybody along the line knowing too much."

Rico reached out with a sneaker and poked Justin's leg under the table. "There's probably a Perry Mason program that deals with that," he said.

Justin gave him a long, steady look, and then turned to Uncle Mike. "So the bottles were transported in grocery sacks?"

"Yes. Someone would come to our baseball games with a grocery bag, as if he'd just been to the store. Isaac wouldn't even see him or talk to him. He'd just tip Calvin off about which player to hit to on his second at-bat. The person with the sack—and it was usually one of the four kids we caught tonight—had a team book, and knew the players. As soon as Calvin hit the ball to a certain player, this person would wander off with the sack and walk to that player's house. Usually there'd be nobody home, because pretty much all the parents come to the games. The teen would hide the bottle in the water barrel—all the houses have water barrels. Later, someone else would pick it up from there."

Rico asked, "How do you know all this now?"

"Isaac's talking. He's made a deal to testify in court if he gets a light sentence and witness protection."

"And the radio station," Hannah said. "Was it the smugglers who were trying to sabotage it?"

"Right. Calvin's been talking too. He happens to be an expert with a Wrist Rocket slingshot."

Justin's jaw dropped. "That's it! That rubber tube I saw hanging out of Calvin's gym bag! It was part of a Wrist Rocket!"

Uncle Mike grinned. "Good eye. Remember, Trent said that Calvin was expert with anything he picked up. That stone in your room, with the message wrapped around it? Calvin had shot it through the window."

Rico's face wore a puzzled frown. "Wait. You didn't find anything in the room when you checked."

His uncle nodded. "My guess is that it must have hit the upper bunk and somehow worked its way between the mattress and the frame. A couple of nights later it fell through and landed on Justin's pillow."

Hannah gasped. "And the radio antenna? Could that have been—"

"Exactly," said Uncle Mike. "Calvin always carried his Wrist Rocket in his gym bag. I let the kids use the Way Station restrooms during the game, and he could have put the slingshot in his belt under his shirt and then strolled around to the other side of the Way Station, as if he was going to use the restroom. From there he could run over to some trees for cover and take aim at the antenna from there."

"That white rag!" Rico said. "Isaac probably went up on the roof earlier and tied the rag to the antenna so Calvin would have a target."

"Right. It probably took him several shots, but those Wrist Rockets are accurate. And Calvin's probably the best shot in town."

"But why," Hannah asked, "would the smugglers want to hurt the radio station?"

"Partly because I always do antidrug promos," said Uncle Mike. "And partly because I'm really pushing the Belize Blockwatch idea, and if everybody gets more alert and reports what they see, that means that the smugglers wouldn't be able to move about as freely. When the baseball broadcasts started, the smugglers probably got even more worried, because they didn't want you boys to innocently broadcast something that would tip off the police about the way the cocaine was being smuggled."

Rico said, "What about that rat in Mary's room? Was that planted?"

"Probably. Maybe one of the teens carried it to the Way Station in the same bag with the Marie Sharp bottle, and just tossed it in her window to pull me away from doing the broadcast."

"What's going to happen to Calvin?" Justin asked.

"He'll be off the team for a while," said Uncle Mike. "He'll probably have to do a bit of community service work—maybe clean the police station for six months without getting paid. And," he said with satisfaction, "he'll probably be getting to know his dad a lot better. Trent's going to spend more time with him."

He raised the empty blender. "Want me to fix some more? No? Hannah, what are your plans? Going back to the farm?"

She shook her head. "Auntie needs me badly here in town. She's going to really twist Father's arm. So maybe I'll still be able to play on the team."

Uncle Mike glanced at Rico and Justin. "And you two— you're heading off toward home tomorrow, right?"

They nodded sadly.

"We got this mystery solved just in time," the man said. "But now you can relax until school starts."

"Not me," Justin said. "Dad's taking me to Africa almost as soon as we get back."

Rico stared. "Africa?"

"Pretty cool, huh? I learned about it in today's e-mail from him. He's doing some articles on policing techniques in other countries. Monique's coming along, too. Her parents have been working at that Kenya dental clinic, and she hasn't seen them for two months."

Rico shuddered. "Glad I'm not going. This trip's been

enough travel for me for a while."

Uncle Mike grinned. "You guys know my e-mail address, right?" he asked. "And you'll keep Hannah and me posted on what you're doing?"

They nodded.

"Because the main thing," he said, "no matter how far away you are, is to keep in touch."

"That's right," Rico said, and he and Justin glanced at each other. "Keep in touch with home."

Since the boys' flight would be early the next morning, Hannah stayed a little longer to talk with them. Uncle Mike promised to drive her to her aunt's house afterward. She and the boys went out to the lobby to talk. Justin told Rico about his conversation with Hannah. As they talk about Bible verses, you play the part of Hannah. Look up each verse and give the answer in your own words.

"What I can't understand," Rico said, "is how does prayer work, really? Is it something like Uncle Mike's broadcast?"

Hannah reached for a Gideon Bible on one of the lobby's end tables. "I think it's a lot simpler than that," she said. "I don't think the prayer has to go very far. Notice what Matthew 28:20 says: _____

_____

_____

"And also John 14:16-18: _____

_____

_____

"There's one thing I've always wondered," Justin said. "If God knows everything already and what's going to happen, why do we even need to pray?"

"First, because He says to," said Hannah. "Look at 1 Thessalonians 5:17: _____

_____

"Second, because Jesus thought it was important enough to teach us how, as you can see in Matthew 6:9-13, the prayer we call 'The Lord's Prayer.' Third, because prayer really does help change things—James 5:16: _____

_____

_____

_____

"Also, Jesus called God 'Father' 200 times. And maybe God just loves to hear us talk to Him."

Rico asked, "Is there anything I can do to make my prayers 'work' better?"

"Sure," Hannah said. "Mark 11:24 says: _____

_____

_____

"Psalm 66:18 says: _____

_____

_____

"Proverbs 28:9 says: _____

_____

_____

"And 1 John 5:14, 15 says: _____

_____

_____

_____

"One more thing," Justin said. "If God doesn't answer my prayer, does that mean He's mad at me?"

Hannah shook her head. "God is like a parent," she said. "He won't give you something that wouldn't be good for you. He likes to give us good gifts. Check out James 1:17:

_____

_____

_____

Discover more about
Justin's real-life
supernatural friend,
Jesus,
by visiting

www.justincaseadventures.org.